TURN THE
CUP AROUND

D0282304

OTHER YEARLING BOOKS YOU WILL ENJOY:

YEARLING BOOKS are designed especially to entertain and enlighten young people. Patricia Reilly Giff, consultant to this series, received her bachelor's degree from Marymount College and a master's degree in history from St. John's University. She holds a Professional Diploma in Reading and a Doctorate of Humane Letters from Hofstra University. She was a teacher and reading consultant for many years, and is the author of numerous books for young readers.

TURN THE CUP AROUND

Barbara Mariconda

A YEARLING BOOK

Published by
Bantam Doubleday Dell Books for Young Readers
a division of
Bantam Doubleday Dell Publishing Group, Inc.
1540 Broadway
New York, New York 10036

Visit us on the Web! www.bdd.com

Educators and librarians, visit the BDD Teacher's
Resource Center at www.bdd.com/teachers

ISBN: 0-440-41311-7

Reprinted by arrangement with Delacorte Press

Printed in the United States of America

September 1998

10 9 8 7 6 5 4 3 2

CWO

In loving memory of Ingrid and Raymond Johnson
and John Schmotzer, S.J.

TURN THE CUP AROUND

Chapter 1
The Eye of the Storm

Dreams are the true interpreters of
our inclinations, but art is required
to sort and understand them.

—Michel de Montaigne (1533–1592)

Even with her eyes shut tight Evie could see the lightning. Each powerful bolt lit up her bedroom in an eerie blue-white light that burst behind her eyelids like the aftermath of a powerful camera flash. The monstrous crackle and boom of thunder followed each flash like a dark, vicious hound snarling down the heels of a cat—a fast and furious white streak of feline.

As the roll of thunder charged along the Maine coast and out to sea, Evie's heart kept pace, pounding in her chest.

"Evie!"

At the sound of her little brother's cry, Evie threw back the covers and leapt from her bed. He called her again. "E-*vie!*"

Gorry, that boy was impatient! She edged, stiff-legged, along the inside wall, far from the windowpanes that creaked and rattled with each crack of thunder.

The wood felt cold under Evie's feet and a shiver ran down her spine. She yanked open her dresser drawer and rummaged in the dark for a pair of socks. Another bolt of lightning hit and was followed by a sharp crack, bringing Evie to the window in spite of herself. She peered out into the night, expecting to see the old apple tree in the yard struck and split in two.

But the gnarly old tree stood right beside the shed as it always had. Its gangly branches waggled in the wind and clawed at the shed like a goblin scratching to get inside. As if in response, the shed door flew open and cracked against the wall.

As Evie turned from the window, something outside caught her eye. First a fleeting shadow, then a small, pale blur, illuminated for a second by another burst of lightning. The shadow seemed humanlike, hunched and awkward, moving swiftly across the lawn. Something about the sight of it made Evie's heart race. She leaned closer to the glass and strained to make out the shape, but whatever it was seemed to have been swallowed up by the darkness.

Jemmy called a third time. "Evie, where are you?"

"I'm coming, Jem!" she yelled. It surprised her to hear how calm her voice sounded. Between all the crashing and booming, she'd half expected it to come out as a tottering squeak. But that would have scared Jemmy even more.

For sure, Evie was scared, but she willed herself to

move. Holding her fear inside was something she was good at.

She slammed the drawer shut, pulled the socks on her feet, and hurried into the hallway.

In less than a few seconds she was in Jemmy's room. He threw himself at her, his legs and arms wrapped around her slender frame like the wisteria vine that wound around the front porch of the house.

She nuzzled her face in his small, freckled neck. She could still detect the faint smell of talcum powder and sweat, and was reminded of the days she'd held him as a baby. Holding him like that caused a feeling so tender to well up inside that Evie had to swallow hard and blink. He was calm now. His Evie was in charge.

When she heard Gram moving about downstairs in the kitchen, Evie hoisted Jemmy onto her hip. At six, he was getting a bit heavy. She shifted him from one hip to the other and made her way toward the stairs. Halfway down the narrow hallway Kirby's door burst open. He stuck his rumpled head of red hair out of the doorway.

"Listen to that thunder!" he shouted. "It's so close I couldn't even count the seconds in between!" His wide-open eyes glowed in the dark like a pair of Ping-Pong balls. He raced out the door and down the stairs, his bathrobe flying behind him like a cape. "I'm gonna go out and watch it from the porch!"

They followed him into the kitchen, where Gram stood, framed in candlelight, the match with a little wisp of smoke swirling off it still in her hand. The flickering light cast shadows across her wrinkled face, making her look older and thinner than she actually was. Kirby headed for the door, all the while looking back over his shoulder from Gram to Evie. Gram stopped him in his tracks with one raised finger. She spoke to Kirby, but it was Evie she was looking at.

"I know what your sister's thinking, and I agree!"

Good. Evie smiled inside and nodded in unspoken agreement. The storm was bad enough, but that shadow, or whatever it was, well . . . there was no *way* she'd let him go out there.

Kirby slumped into a chair, defeated. "I'm not a baby. I'm eight years old! You two never let me do anything fun," he muttered.

Gram patted him on the shoulder. "This is some ugly storm we're having. You'd best stay inside."

Evie shook her head and stared at her brother. "I don't know how you ever became the daredevil of the family," she said. But even as she said it, she couldn't help thinking that she knew *exactly* how Kirby became such a daredevil. Their mother had died right after Jemmy was born. Complications from childbirth was how Gram explained it. When you'd lost your mother at just barely two, as Kirby had, there wasn't a whole lot left to be afraid of.

"What about we all sit down and wait out the storm?" asked Gram. Another flash of lightning bathed the kitchen in light. It looked, for a fraction of a second, like it was morning.

Evie jumped a little and shut her eyes tight, trying to

4

hang on to that split-second image of morning in that cozy room. The kitchen, fragrant with nutmeg and all-spice, Gram's linseed oil and oil paint, was usually Evie's favorite place in the house. As a matter of fact, in the six years since they'd arrived here, this kitchen had always felt safe and welcoming. But tonight even those familiar, comforting things felt unsettling and peculiar.

Try as she might, Evie could not bring to mind a single clear image of her old house—the house she'd once lived in with her parents.

Shoot, it seemed like those first six years of her life belonged to someone else entirely. Evie's earliest memories were of life here at the inn, helping Gram run the place and looking after the boys.

Sometimes, if she strained hard enough, Evie could almost bring to mind what she'd come to think of as her "other life." Dim, golden-edged images—her mother's pretty face, her father's smile, a glimpse of soft moss-colored wallpaper with puffy pink sheep grazing, a swing-set in a neat green yard—all these scraps of memories seemed blurred and far away.

Mostly, Evie regarded these bits and pieces as a kind of stubborn memory game that teased her from time to time. But other times, when lying in bed, almost asleep, she'd try to bring the faded pictures into focus. And she found that the more she yearned to remember her mother's face, to hear her father's voice, the more blurred and distant these memories became.

This did not make Evie sad. Her mother had been dead

and her father off in that hospital, too sick to leave, *way* too long for her to feel sadness. And questions about her father's illness seemed to unsettle her grandmother. Gram had always made it clear that he was too sick for young visitors and that seeing him would be upsetting.

So Evie'd worked hard at pushing her questions aside. Now, in the place where all those questions had been, all Evie felt was a space. A gap. And it seemed that the only way to avoid falling in was to be careful and stay *far* away from the edge. From time to time, Evie still played this stubborn, no-win game, always grasping for something that just didn't seem to be there. But what was the use, anyway?

Gram motioned for them to sit. "So, how about a cup of coffee? Some cookies and milk? The 'lectricity is out, but our trusty old stove works, rain or shine!"

Evie nodded yes to the coffee and went about getting cookies and milk for the boys. She watched Gram take out an old tin coffeepot, dented here and there, with a little glass dome on the top. Gram filled it with coffee, water, and a pinch of salt, and set it on the gas jet of the ancient stove. Evie stared at the glass dome on top for a few minutes before she saw the small streams of amber-colored liquid spurting up like a geyser. After a few minutes the amber turned a rich brown—raw sienna, was how Gram described it—and then Evie knew the coffee was done.

The boys slurped milk and dunked cookies, and Evie and Gram sipped coffee with cream.

"Evie, would you get the soomp ready?" asked Gram.

6

Jemmy jumped up and down and tugged at her sleeve.

"Oh, Evie-Jevie, do my cup first!" he pleaded. He did a little jig around the table. "Please! Evie, get me a cup, and Kirby too!"

Evie got out two more cups and saucers and took the coffeepot from the stove. She knew the ritual by heart and went about it despite the darkness in the room.

Evie finished all but the last tiny sip of coffee in her cup and poured a small drop in each of the clean cups for Jemmy and Kirby. She removed the rickety top of the old tin pot and spooned a small glop of coffee grounds into each of their cups—just as she'd seen Gram do a thousand times. She and Jemmy turned the cups around and around in their hands, swirling the grounds in the re-maining coffee. Then they turned their cups upside down, setting them on their saucers to drain. Gram and Kirby did the same.

Evie's cup was first. Gram held the delicate porcelain lightly in her long, knobby-knuckled fingers. As she turned the cup around, her fingers sent thin, spiderlike shadows scurrying across the wall. In the flickering can-dlelight and occasional flashes of lightning, everything in the kitchen suddenly looked cold, sharp, and unfamiliar.

Evie shivered. She was fascinated, as always, watching Gram study the speckled patterns of coffee grounds cast like stars around the inside of the cup. It was amazing how the "soomp," as Gram called it, supposedly turned the bottom of the cup into a crystal ball, out of which she spelled their fortunes. For a moment those specks and clumps reminded Evie of the back of Jemmy's freckled neck. It was a cozy thought.

Gram tilted her head a little, this way and that, and turned Evie's cup around and around in her hands. Then she paused and the faint smile on her lips disappeared. Evie saw a deep crease form along her grandmother's brow and the edges of her mouth tighten. Then, with the slightest shake of her head, the dark expression vanished—just like the phantom shadow Evie had seen earlier in the yard. If Evie hadn't been watching carefully, she'd have missed it altogether. But she *had* seen it. She knew Gram saw something in the cup. Something bad. Something she didn't want to share.

In an attempt to find something she could reveal, Gram turned the cup again, just as Evie knew she would.

"Ayuh," Gram whispered, pointing, "now we've got something." She made tiny clucking sounds with her tongue as she took in and sorted through the signs and symbols in the cup.

The boys leaned forward in their chairs, staring at the small brown clumps of coffee grounds, and hung on Gram's every word.

"What do you see, Grammy?" asked Jemmy, practically climbing into his grandmother's lap.

Evie pushed her uneasiness aside and smirked at her brothers.

"Don't you know that this is all in fun?" she asked. "There's no such thing as a *real* fortune in there." She pointed toward the cup in Gram's hand. "They're *coffee* grounds, Jemmy," she said, rolling her eyes. "Wet, soggy coffee grounds, that's all!"

Just saying it made her feel better. There were no amazing answers nestled among those soggy coffee grounds, that was for sure. How could there be? Nobody ever asked questions that *really* mattered, anyway. They all knew that some things were better left alone.

"Evie's just making that up, isn't she, Grammy?" asked Jemmy, his eyebrows raised like two giant question marks. He was so serious, Evie thought she might just laugh out loud.

"What do *you* think," said Kirby to his brother. "Of *course* she's makin' it up! Just read the fortune, Gram!"

Gram glanced at Evie and went back to studying the cup. "Ayuh," she said again, tapping the cup with a crooked finger. "A web. A spider's web."

Evie fought to contain her surprise at Gram's words. Was it just a coincidence that only a moment ago she'd been thinking of a spider—of the shadow spider, scurrying along the wall in the candlelight, cast by her grandmother's hands? Gram squinted into the cup as if to bring the image into better focus, and nodded again in that knowing way she had. "And there she is, that able little weaver, spinning a new web."

"But what does it *mean*, Gram?" Kirby asked.

Gram considered for a moment. Evie picked up a cookie she didn't really want, twisted it apart, and concentrated on scraping off the white filling with her teeth. She could feel her grandmother gazing intently at her.

9

"A busy spider, a new web—it stands for *change,* that's what. Or perhaps some new spin on an old tale." She paused, then continued in a more serious tone. "It could mean our Evie will be facing a new chapter in her life story."

Gram nodded, convinced. Evie's thoughts drifted, lulled by the tide rushing in, crashing over the low-lying rocks in the cove beyond the yard. Life was a lot like that, Evie thought, like the tides, or like their summer house-guests, in and out like clockwork. She didn't much believe in new chapters, or new spins on old tales. She yawned. It was time to head back to bed. The summer people would be arriving tomorrow, and there'd be plenty of cleaning up to do after this storm to get things ready.

She stood, stretched, and absentmindedly kissed Gram goodnight. Evie couldn't help noticing that Gram was still clutching the cup in her hand.

"One more thing," Gram said. The unusually sharp tone of her voice stopped Evie short.

Gram tapped the cup. "A web is easy to get tangled in. Tangled up—captured—caught!" She paused. "So, be careful! *Think* about what you're doing! Be responsible and be cautious!"

Evie nodded quickly and left the room, carefully avoiding her grandmother's eyes. Her face felt hot and she was surprised at the hurt and anger that welled up inside her. Why in the world would Gram feel she had to tell her about being responsible? Gram, of all people, knew how careful she was, how responsible she was for a twelve-year-old!

Gram's words still stung as Evie paused at her bedroom window and glanced outside. She leaned forward and strained her eyes, still hoping to define the shadowy figure she'd seen earlier.

As she squinted, the yard beyond the window blurred and her eyes focused instead on the space just inside the window frame. She was shocked to see that it was now crisscrossed with a network of angel-fine threads over which a dark, nimble spider skillfully worked, encasing a small, helpless insect in a suffocating silken bag. It *couldn't* have been there before. How could she have missed it, right there—an inch in front of her nose?

She raised her hand to swat at the spider, but pulled back at the dewy, sticky feel of the web against her fingers. She backed into bed and lay there with her eyes wide open, determined to keep careful track of the spider. Somewhere before dawn her eyes closed and she fell into an uneasy sleep. In the morning when she woke up, only the faintest trace of the web remained.

And the spider was gone.

Chapter 2
The Descent

Sketch pad in her hand, Evie stepped out the back door. The air had a clear, crisp, balsam smell, as though the pines along the shore had been thoroughly washed and hung up in the ocean breeze to dry. She stretched her arms up over her head and inhaled deeply. The world felt fresh and new, as it always did after a storm. Evie felt the same way. Last night's fear seemed silly now. It seemed to have been swept out to sea with the thunderclouds.

"Mornin'."

Evie turned toward the clipped, twangy voice. Pop, dressed as always in his well-pressed blue dickies and cap, already had a screwdriver in his hand, and was refitting the hinges on the shed door.

"Hi, Pop," she said, making her way across the lawn. She watched him turn the screwdriver neatly in his hand, scowling at the hinge as if it had behaved badly. What would they do without Pop? Evie wondered. He was much more than a neighbor; he did odd jobs around the inn, painting, yard work, carpentry—whatever needed to be done. And after a storm like last night's, there was plenty that needed doing.

Pop shook his head and whistled softly through his teeth. "Ayuh, it was a helluva storm last night, it was." He put one final twist on the hinge and stood back to examine his handiwork. "Still, I can't for the life of me figure how it ripped this door off its hinge. She was ship-shape in the spring when I checked her last."

Evie stood silent. Pop didn't expect an answer. He was thinking, was all. Pop took off his cap and wiped it across his forehead. A small tuft of his gray hair rustled in the salty breeze. "And what do you make of this?"

He bent down, pulled a wrinkled bag out of the shed, and emptied its contents on the ground. A dozen empty, dented tuna fish cans, their lids peeled crudely back; several dried, shriveled tubes of oil paint; a large, filthy shirt; and an assortment of rags fell at her feet.

"It's a bag of garbage," said Evie. What was he getting at, anyway?

Pop picked the stuff up and shoved it back in the bag.

13

"Found it on the floor of the shed," he said. "It warn't there a week ago." He scratched at his head, messing up his small fluff of flyaway hair. "I think someone's been out here, that's what I think."

Evie thought of the shadow she'd seen last night. The shadow that had been moving across the yard. She opened her mouth to mention it, then stopped. She twirled a strand of her long blond hair around and around her finger and nibbled her bottom lip. She'd seen something out there last night, but *what*?

Didn't matter. Pop was already moving down the walk, depositing the bag of junk in the barrel behind the house.

Evie strolled along the walk toward the front yard. Yech! She wrinkled her nose as she spotted the number of swollen, waterlogged worms on the pathway. Disgusting. She stepped gingerly around them. By noon they'd be crispy, dark squiggles that Pop would sweep away into the grass. They all worked hard to keep the place looking well kept and respectable. Evie pulled back a large limb that had fallen across the sign on the front lawn. She pulled the bushy pine branch aside to uncover the neat green letters—COZY COVE BED AND BREAKFAST.

Evie dragged the branch along the walk toward Pop's compost pile behind the garden. Its bristly needles scratched at her, causing a prickly feeling along her arms and legs. She turned, stretched her arms out far, leaned over, and backed along the walkway in an attempt to move the branch without letting it touch her skin. She noticed that giving the branch an occasional push-pull, side-to-side sweep cleared the waterlogged worms right off the path. She counted them as she swept them aside. "One, two, three, four . . ."

One stubborn worm, probably squashed on the concrete, clung to the walk. "Come *on*!" she said, giving the pine branch a sturdier push. It stuck for a second, and then let go, causing Evie to topple to one side. "Stupid, lousy worms!" she yelled.

Just before Evie hit the ground a pair of hands broke her fall. She regained her footing, spun around and found herself looking into the spectacled eyes of a stranger.

"Have a problem with worms, do you?" he asked. He had light brown hair and clear blue eyes. Something about those eyes made Evie's heart beat a little faster. He might have been teasing her, but he wore such a serious expression that Evie wasn't sure how to answer. His eyes held her, awkward and tongue-tied, and she could feel her face turning red. By the time she opened her mouth, the man had nodded, turned, and was heading up the steps. She stared after him.

"He's an odd one," said Pop. She hadn't realized Pop had made his way back up the walk.

"Who is he?" she asked.

"He's the new houseguest," Pop told her. "The professor. Your grandmother's renting to him for the whole summer."

They watched him carry his worn leather bag up the stairs. Despite the man's thin frame and the large size of the bag, he seemed to lift it with no effort at all.

"Met him out by the road, I did," said Pop. "Quiet. A little uppity, I think." He nodded as if he'd just rethought the whole thing and heartily agreed with his first impression. "No car, no cab, he was just walkin' up the road with that beat-up old bag in his hand. His clothes looked a tad wet, like he'd been out in that storm. I said hello and he just looks at me through them fancy glasses and barely nods. Said his car broke down back on Route One. Don't know what to make of him."

"What kind of professor is he?" asked Evie. She wondered what a professor thought of a girl who talked to worms.

"Damned if I know," said Pop with a shrug.

Evie sat on the step and watched the door close behind the professor. She hadn't liked the idea of Gram renting to one person for the entire summer. She'd always liked the guests coming and going, coming and going. It was more interesting that way. If someone was crabby, or dull, well . . . they were gone in a day or two, or in a week on the outside. But this year, Gram had decided it would be less work to rent for the entire season.

Evie looked out across to the Dearborn place, barely visible between the trees. The Dearborn family, including Evie's best friend, Eliza, would be in Florida for most of the summer, staying with Eliza's sick grandmother. So now, besides missing Eliza, she'd be stuck with whoever came to the Cozy Cove for the season—the unsmiling professor, and some family called the Elliots.

Just then the boys appeared.

16

"Come on, Evie," Kirby said. "Let's go out and see if the storm took down any trees out by the rocks!" It was as good an idea as any, so Evie followed them on down the walk.

Gram called after them, "Be *careful* over to those rocks! Do you hear me?"

"We will!" they yelled. So she was still on that careful kick, thought Evie, all because of that peculiar fortune last night.

Evie pushed her discomfort aside and grabbed the tin buckets on the steps. "Since we're going out, we may as well pick some blueberries on the way. Here," she said, "each of you grab a bucket!"

They each took one and headed around the opposite side of the house, across the yard and over to the blueberry bushes. They combed the bushes for the plump, silvery-blue berries. Jemmy always picked the most, but wound up with the least in his bucket, and today was no different. Evie watched him jam his mouth full to overflowing with berries. Small streams of purplish juice dribbled down his wrists and his mouth had a bluish ring around it. The boy had no manners whatsoever. None at all.

"You'll give yourself another stomachache, you gannet-gut," said Evie. Jemmy kept right on nibbling. Evie and Kirby filled their buckets and set them aside to pick up on the way back. Kirby led the way down the dirt path leading into the woods. Before long Evie felt the familiar spongy feeling of a hundred years' worth of pine needles underfoot. They always just naturally hushed up on this part of the walk, and Evie often wondered if the soft, cushiony sounds of their footsteps maybe snuck up their legs and muffled their tongues. The sun filtering through the trees sent down dappled patterns of light that danced across the forest floor at their feet. Evie was always surprised at the occasional sea urchin, mussel, or oyster shell nestled among the pine needles, probably carried into the woods, picked clean, and dropped by a hungry gull. It reminded her that no matter where they walked, the ocean was never far away.

They continued up an embankment, still shaded and protected by trees. This was the best part of the walk, for sure. All of a sudden the trees just seemed to lean back and give way to nothing but blue sky. Beyond the trees, all bowed back from the wind off the ocean, was a huge ledge of solid gray rock that dropped off in gradual steep steps, protecting the coast of Maine from the Atlantic Ocean. Waves crashed against it, and the rocks, like giant dinosaurs left behind from the Ice Age, didn't retreat an inch. The wind whipped in off the ocean, sending Evie's long, straight hair back off her face at the same angle as the bowing, windswept trees on the summit.

Evie paused for a moment right at the spot where the forest floor turned to stone. It was like entering a new land, a foreign country, and she liked to stand still and take it all in.

Kirby and Jemmy barreled on ahead, in search of small tidal pools and other treasures that the sea had left behind. Evie watched them go, and set off for a good spot to settle down. Hard as it was, the stone was often marked by smooth dips and curves that made perfect places to set your backside down on. Evie walked, her eyes scanning the water, watching the whitecapped waves. The waves, working their way on in, still had a ways to go before high tide. Perfect. As long as the tide wasn't all the way in, there'd be plenty good places to sit and sketch.

Evie made her way down, making sure that the boys were still in sight. She wanted to find a new spot, a new angle where she could capture, or at least *try* to capture, the beauty of Coleman's Cove. She pulled the pencil from the binding of her pad and stuck it behind her ear.

Then she saw it—an interesting dip—down a ways and off to her right. The light looked just right there, reflecting off of a funny outcropping of brush that she'd never noticed before.

Evie moved swiftly, looking forward to that small thrill of excitement she always felt when she found just the right spot to sketch from. She moved across the rock and into the sunlight, her eyes fixed on the spot up ahead.

Which was why she never saw the narrow crevice beneath her feet, drastic and steep. By the time she saw it, it was too late. The small space between the rocks was just large enough, just hungry enough, to suck her in and swallow her whole.

Chapter 3

Trapped!

Evie's scream was lost in the deep, narrow walls of stone that surrounded her. Her heart pounded in her chest. Godfrey Mighty, what had happened? One minute she'd been basking in sunlight, the next, plunged into darkness. The space between the rocks was too narrow to allow her to actually tumble. Instead, she slid in an upright position, scraping her back, legs, and arms, until her feet hit something solid.

She grasped at the wall of the cave and immediately yanked her hand back from the cool, slick stone.

"Kirby! Jemmy!"

Evie barely recognized the sound of her own voice. Its thin hollowness sent ripples of gooseflesh along her bare arms. A mocking, teasing imitation echoed eerily back. The air wrapped around her, moist and heavy, and a mix of saltwater and mildew stung at her nose. Evie gulped to force down the lump that had risen in her throat and took several deep breaths to hold off her rising panic.

She opened her mouth to call out and shut it again. Why even bother? They'd *never* hear her. And on top of it, she'd promised Gram a million times that she wouldn't let her brothers explore the rocks alone, that she'd be right there looking out for them. And where were they now? Off on their own somewhere. How long would it be before they realized she was gone and come looking for her? Would they notice her sketch pad lying on the rocks, its pages shuffled and whipped around by the wind? She thought of the two of them, traipsing across the cliffs, all taken up in their make-believe and exploring, and decided that she couldn't count on their coming back for her any time soon.

Evie squinted into the blackness, her eyes struggling to adjust to the dark. After what seemed like forever, she realized that she was not in total darkness. A thin sliver of light crept in overhead. In fact, that thin shaft of light lit up the steep crevice into which she'd slipped.

The sight of that steep incline sent her heart racing again. Slipping down between those rocks had been easy. Climbing back out would be impossible.

Evie slumped against the wall of rock, ignoring the thin layer of slime that oozed against her back. She opened her mouth to call out again, but could not find her voice. She felt strangled and paralyzed with fear and totally helpless. Covering her face with her hands, Evie willed her heart to slow down. She *had* to think. She had to *do* something. She opened her eyes and tried to get a grasp on her surroundings. As she strained her eyes and ears she became aware of a faint, vaguely familiar rhythmic sound. Gorry, what was that sound anyway? She closed her eyes again, trying to place the deep, repetitious swoosh and hiss.

Suddenly, she knew the sound, knew it as surely as she knew her own name. It was the surf—stubborn and forceful, pounding its way against the walls of stone that protected the coastline from the crashing sea. It brought to mind a pendulum—the one in the old clock at home by the stairway. The tide was exactly like that, swinging in against the cliffs, each stroke bringing the surf in higher, filling in the small, empty spaces between the rocks—the small, empty places that could gobble up a girl and hold her there, captive and terrified.

The sound of the tide coming closer was interrupted by a scuffling sound. "Oh God, tell me it's not a rat!" She pushed away the memory of the fat water rat she'd seen one day last spring scurrying between the rocks. The thought of meeting that ugly rodent there in the dark nudged her forward. She walked slowly at first, carefully placing one foot in front of the other, her hands groping, swimming in the darkness, feeling her way through to what she hoped might be an escape route.

Evie listened closely as she went. Was the sound of the surf getting louder? Was the misty spray of the ocean settling on her face just her imagination, or could it be that the pounding sea *was* only seconds away, ready to crash over the walls of stone surrounding her?

It was the first time she thought about drowning, and realized she could actually *die* out there. It made no sense, dying like that. Evie gulped at the panic rising in her throat.

"*Mommy!*" The word escaped her trembling lips on its own, from some hidden place deep inside, as if to remind her that senseless deaths *did* in fact happen. She couldn't remember the last time she'd called her mother's name out loud, and the sound and feel of it touched a place in her that she normally kept buried safely away. Unsettled and vaguely angry, Evie inhaled shakily, determined to regain her resolve.

"Move!" she told herself. "Move!"

Then, for a moment, she forgot about the tide, she forgot about her mother, and she forgot about escape.

Because what Evie saw looming up in front of her, out of place and bigger than life, caught her up and held her there, frozen, dead in her tracks.

Chapter 4
The Image

The wide shaft of sunlight cut through the darkness up ahead, lighting up the flat wall of stone.

Evie took a few hesitant steps closer. The wall had this odd, silvery glow, probably, she thought, from the harsh angle of the sun hitting it.

And there in the middle of the wall of stone, an image jumped out. It was an image of a cat, a white cat with mismatched eyes—one blue, the other green. Evie thought at first that it was just a coincidence—that the rough surface of the stone along with her runaway imagination had only *suggested* the cat, but as she got closer she saw that that was not the case. The cat seemed so real that Evie could swear it was watching her.

It was a painting, Evie was sure. She approached it, and on closer view saw the careful brushstrokes creating the cat's graceful whiskers and soft white fur. And, most peculiar of all—the painting was labeled! Just below the cat's face were three scrawled letters—C A T.

Evie reached out and ran her finger ever so gently along the cat's face. She was shocked to discover that the paint was still wet! Evie rubbed her fingers together and stared at the smudge of paint. It was oil paint—she knew the smell and feel of it by heart. It was the same kind of paint Gram used for her landscapes and seascapes, back home in their sunny kitchen.

A gurgling sound, followed by the swoosh and hiss of the surf, turned Evie's attention away from the cat. It wouldn't be long before the tide rushed in. It occurred to her that if someone had recently painted here, that they *must* have found a way back out.

She stole a look back at the painting as a small amount of water foamed and bubbled around her feet.

Without hesitating another second, Evie ran into the light, knowing that the sea was not far behind.

Just beyond the painting was an opening—a carved-out space between a U-shaped outcropping of rock through which Evie could see the bright blue sky above her.

Her heart swelled in excitement and her pulse quickened. This might be a way out. She squinted into the sun, and stumbled forward, sizing up the rock formations for a spot she could scale.

Shoot! There wasn't a single ledge or foothold she could

reach. The stone was set mostly in vertical fashion, straight up and down, and it was slick to the touch.

And then she saw it. A tree—actually, the sea-ravaged remains of a scrubby pine, its branches long gone, stripped and snapped off by the sea. Around the trunk, small stumps stuck out in circular patterns, marking the places where the branches once had been. The bark had been torn back and eaten away, leaving the trunk worn down to a smooth, pale gray.

The top of the tree was wedged against the craggy summit of stone above her, and the bottom was sunk deep between the muck-covered stone at her feet. It had probably been tossed there by a violent winter storm, but to Evie it had been placed there by the hands of an angel.

"Yes," she whispered. The sound that fell from her lips was as much a sigh of relief as it was a word. She ran to her makeshift ladder and grabbed hold. The stumps made perfect handles and footholds, and Evie scrambled up as easily as a monkey.

At the top, she heaved herself over the edge and dragged herself up onto the warm, dry stone. She lay there a minute, facedown on the rock, her heart pounding against her chest, and let the sun chase the chill clear out of her.

Evie sat up and glanced down for one last look at the cat, staring after her. Then the surf surged in, swirling around and lapping at the cat's chin, nose, and finally the mismatched eyes. Evie blinked and stared at the spot where the cat had been. All that was left was a ghost, a phantom outline of the cat, fading into the wall of rock. It was the oddest thing she'd ever seen, that was for sure. She turned, and a shiver ran down her spine as she looked out over Coleman's Cove, trying to get her bearings. She couldn't shake the feeling that she'd been somewhere else, somewhere far from home, when in fact she'd been between the familiar rocks she'd climbed across and explored since she was able to walk. There was no sign of her sketch pad whatsoever.

"Evie!"

She swung around and headed in the direction of Jemmy's voice. The sound of the little pest caused a surprising lump to form in her throat. I will *not* cry, she told herself, and took a deep, shaky breath. After all, they counted on her to be in charge.

She saw them then, the wind tossing their hair and throwing their high-pitched voices out to sea. When she got closer, she could see that Jemmy was near tears himself. Kirby looked angry, his small mouth pulled in a tight line. Shoot. Thanks to her they were scared and probably good and mad too.

"It wasn't nice that you went and hided on us!" Jemmy's bottom lip trembled a little and he stuck it out, obviously trying to cover up his fear with a big dose of anger.

"I wasn't *hiding*," said Evie. She reached out for Jemmy

27

and he pulled away from her. Great. She could almost see the stubborn tears running down his cheeks and dripping off his nose.

"Then where *were* you?"

Kirby's voice didn't waver a bit. He was *really* mad and—although he'd never admit it—worried.

"I wasn't hiding," said Evie again. "I fell and slipped down between the rocks. There was kind of a cave down there, all dark and wet. It took me a long time to find my way out."

Jemmy wiped his face on his forearm and turned to face her. Kirby's eyebrows shot up. This was even better than a nasty little game of hide-and-seek, that was for sure. Evie could see that they smelled an adventure.

Pleased to see that they were no longer mad, she launched into an account of her ordeal. But when she got to the part about the cat, she paused. It wasn't time to share that—not just yet, anyway. She needed to think it through and make some sense out of it first. Besides, there'd be no way of keeping the boys away from that spot once they heard about the painting. And now that the painting had washed away, who would believe her?

The boys stared at her openmouthed. She'd earned a new level of respect in their eyes, that much she could see.

"Let's go back there so you can show us where it is!" Kirby's face was flushed with excitement. His eyes darted past her toward the higher rocks.

"It's dangerous over there," said Evie angrily. "I'm not going to have you falling in the way I did!"

"Evie . . . ," Kirby begged.

"I'll take you there another time," she said, "if you can keep quiet about it and promise, absolutely promise you won't ever try to go there alone!"

"But—" began Kirby.

"Do you promise, or not?" she demanded.

Kirby sighed. "I promise."

Evie turned to Jemmy. "What about you?"

He nodded solemnly. "Promise."

"And not one word about this to Gram," Evie cautioned, "you hear me? If she finds out, it'll be the last time we go exploring!"

They nodded, all straight-faced and serious, and followed Evie back over the rocks, through the pine forest and blueberry bushes, and on across the front yard.

As they went, Evie made a silent vow to keep the painting a secret until all of her questions were answered. Somehow she'd find out who had painted it—and why.

Chapter 5
Safe Haven

The screen door banged shut behind them as they made their way into the kitchen.

Gram had been busy, Evie could see, as she was every day at this time. A bowl of blueberries had been washed and set by the sink waiting to be baked into muffins or turnovers, or made into jam. Gram had her paints spread out on the table and a new canvas on her easel. The professor sat across from her, glancing over his newspaper, watching Gram paint. He nodded to Evie; she nodded back and followed his gaze again to Gram's canvas.

A small, peculiar thought snaked through Evie's head— could *Gram* have painted that cat? Evie stared at her grandmother. She had the ability, that was for sure, but when could she possibly have done it? And why?

Gram looked up suddenly.

"Evie, sweet, stop staring. It's not polite." Evie looked away. But not before she noticed the wrinkled tubes of oil paint spread across the table. The same kind of tubes Pop had shown her out in the shed.

Gram was already back to her painting.

"So, how're my kids?" Gram asked without looking up.

"Okay," Evie said, making her way to the sink to wash herself up a little. She was glad Gram was busy with her painting. Otherwise she'd notice her dirty hands and scraped legs. The professor noticed, though.

"Looks like you've been roughing it up a bit," he said. "Were you out exploring on those rocks?"

Evie plunged her hands in the sink to wash away the telltale dirt and avoided his gaze. "Just hanging around," she said. Jeez, just when she'd gotten past Gram the professor had to go sticking his nose where it didn't belong. She peeked over her shoulder at her grandmother dipping her grizzled paintbrush in a baby food jar caked with thinning oil paint and full of linseed oil. She hadn't paid any attention, thank goodness. She was too caught up in her work. Could she actually be the mystery painter?

No, it wasn't possible. Gram had been at the Cozy Cove the whole time. Unless . . . Evie thought of the shadow in the yard last night. Could that have been Gram returning from the cave? Could she have dropped the used tubes of paint and soiled shirt in the shed in her hurry to get back inside?

No, it was absurd—her grandmother out in the dark in a raging storm. Impossible. But if not Gram, then who?

Gram peered at her latest painting and mopped a strand of fluffy, faded hair off of her forehead, leaving a streak of blue paint in its place. She sold her paintings to the summer people who fell in love with her quiet part of the Maine coast and longed to take a little bit of its charm back home to the suburbs with them. It seemed that as soon as Evie got used to seeing a pretty picture hanging in the hall or over the mantel, someone would cart it off to Boston or New York or who knows where. Which was another reason Gram wouldn't be wasting her time painting pictures in caves.

Evie suddenly thought of her art teacher, Julia. Julia was a little offbeat, and she was always roaming, sketching, out on the rocks. Maybe Julia had been the artist. It was a thought.

Jemmy stretched a dirty hand up toward the blueberry bowl, his eyes as wide open as that pit of a stomach he had.

"Hey!"

Evie and Gram had yelled together, causing Jemmy to jump. The professor jumped too. They all laughed at that.

"Nothin' else for you, Jemmy," said Gram, "or you'll spoil your dinner and your supper too." She pronounced the words "din-nuh" and "sup-puh." Jemmy pouted a little and edged his way along the kitchen counter, scoping out the fixings for later.

Over by the dish drainer Evie noticed the breakfast tray, stacked high with dirty dishes. They had to get done sometime, and Gram was liable to leave them, especially if she was really taken up in her new painting. Evie moved the tray over near the sink, with Jemmy trailing behind her like a puppy, and turned on the tap to rinse off the dishes.

"Wait!"

Jemmy grabbed hold of Evie's arm, sending the stack of china plates in her hand clattering into the sink.

"Jeremy Raymond Johannson!"

He froze. Gram only used their full names when she really meant business.

"Why in heaven's name are you gaffling onto my fine china?"

Jemmy started jigging about a little. He always did that when he got excited. Or when he waited too long to use the toilet. This time it was probably a little bit of both. "Evie was gonna rinse out them dishes and there's plenty of perfec'ly good soomp in there!"

He pointed his grubby finger at the coffee cups.

Evie laughed. It wasn't enough for Gram to read their *own* fortunes. Now he wanted his fortune read from someone *else's* soomp.

"If she reads you from somebody else's soomp, you might wind up with their fortune instead of your own!"

Evie grinned a sly grin and raised an eyebrow. Jemmy pulled his hand back as though the cup contained poison.

"Nonsense!" Gram didn't tolerate much teasing. She stood, picked up one of the cups and handed it to Jemmy. "The fortune belongs to whoever *turns* the cup around," she said.

He hesitated for a second, shot Evie and Kirby a sassy look, and began turning the cup around and around in his chubby little hands.

"Over the sink," said Evie, shaking her head. He was dripping coffee all over the floor.

He thrust the cup at Gram, still doing that little jig. The professor put his paper aside. "So," he said to Gram, "you're a fortune-teller as well as an artist?"

Gram smiled. "Hand me your cup, Professor, and I'll tell you whatever you'd like to know." In answer, the professor raised an eyebrow and smiled a lopsided smile.

Jemmy was getting impatient. He tugged at Gram's sleeve. "What do you see, Grammy?" Gorry, he could hardly wait.

Gram smiled at him and pointed into the cup. "What do *you* see?" she asked.

Jemmy squinted and screwed up his little face. His tongue stuck out one corner of his mouth. Gosh, he was so serious, it was hard to keep a straight face.

All of a sudden his eyes opened wide and he broke into a big smile. His eyebrows lifted in two reddish arches.

"A cat!" he shouted. "I see a cat! A white cat!"

It was as if he'd thrown himself against Evie with all his might and knocked the wind right out of her. She tried, too late, to stifle the gasp that escaped her lips.

They all looked at her, their eyebrows raised in a question. Godfrey Mighty, what made him say that?

Evie stammered for a second. "W-Well," she said, avoiding their eyes, "it's just that all I see there is a big brown clump. I don't see how a *brown* clump could be a *white* cat." Even as she said the words "white cat" she felt those eyes, one blue, one green, staring at her. She knew she sounded silly, but it was the best she could do to cover her amazement. It was hard enough to try to keep her face from turning scarlet, and to quiet her heart so that its thundersome thumping wouldn't give her away.

"It *was* white," said Jemmy stubbornly. "It was white with one eye green and one eye blue."

"*Jemmy!*" Kirby looked about ready to wallop him one.

Jemmy stepped back a little and looked at Gram. The professor looked from one of them to the other, obviously enjoying the whole scene.

"It was following us around the rocks while we were looking for . . ."

"Tide pools!" Kirby was practically shouting. "We were looking for tide pools out on the rocks."

Evie let out a silent sigh. That Kirby was quick. Her secret was safe for now. But her brothers had seen the cat—a *real* cat with mismatched eyes. And they hadn't even mentioned it to her!

"We tried to catch the kitty," said Jemmy. "Me and

Kirby wanted to bring the kitty home." Jeez, that boy didn't know when to keep quiet!

Kirby rolled his eyes. Gram was giving them a look, all right.

"You know we can't keep a cat," said Gram. "Some of the guests might be allergic."

"But . . . ," began Jemmy.

Gram pointed back to the cup. "So, what about this?" she said, tapping at the cup. "A cat." She studied the cup again. "Ayuh, I see it too." She nodded her head and tightened her lips. "Cats are cautious, careful creatures," she said. "They have nine lives. You only have one." She gazed up at them, suddenly serious. "That's the message here today. Be careful and cautious and watchful as a cat!"

Gram put Jemmy's cup aside and turned, and motioned for Evie's cup.

But Evie already had her cup at the sink. She took one last look at the soomp in the bottom, turned the water on full force, and watched the water wash the images out of her cup, out of her mind, and down the drain.

Chapter 6
Sweet Dreams?

The small bird was perched just out of reach. It called out to her.

"Evie, Evie."

The voice didn't seem to belong to the bird at all. It was surprisingly deep and hauntingly familiar. Evie knew she'd heard that voice before, and the fact that she couldn't place it caused a tight knot to form in her gut. She shifted the large bag that she carried from one hand to the other and offered the bird some seed. Then she grasped the bulky bag in both hands again.

This bag she'd been given was just too heavy to carry. Her shoulders ached from the effort. If only she could find her *mother. She knew her mother could carry it. Her mother would know just what to do.*

"Mommy!"

Evie called out but there was no answer. The silence taunted her. Why wasn't anybody listening? Only the small bird cocked its head quizzically to one side, as though just as confused as Evie. It was more than any six-year-old could bear.

Then she remembered. Her mother was dead. The recollection made her grow even weaker, and the light around her faded. The walls began closing in on all sides. Closer and closer they loomed, at crazy angles, so close that the room grew dark and menacingly stuffy. Evie gasped in the suffocating dimness that closed around her like a coffin.

Suddenly the bird began to change. It grew bigger and bigger until it was twice Evie's size. Its gentle eyes turned marblelike and its small beak grew large and hooked. Evie backed up but there was no escape. The huge, hawklike bird grasped her in its sharp talons and carried her off. Terror-stricken, she stared into the bird's cold blue eyes and winced as its sharp talons pressed into her skin.

Then they were no longer flying. Evie watched in horrible fascination as the bird mutated still again. Its talons transformed before her eyes, splitting and stretching, two becoming four, and the reptilian skin turned dark and metallic. Cold, shiny glass balls materialized in the lifeless talons and the bird's powerful wingspan spread and solidified, its tawny feathers disappearing into the woodgrain of a circular oak table top. The long tail feather leaned forward and a thick wooden pedestal sprang up in its place, supporting what had become a timeworn dining table.

Evie crouched below the table, unable to breathe. A terrible crash was followed by the sound of shattering glass. There was screaming, and she knew with sudden and sickening clarity what the crash had been. Oh God, she knew—and it was her fault.

It had been Kirby! He'd dropped his bottle and fallen out of his high chair. She was supposed to be watching him. But she'd been so concerned about the bird that she hadn't been paying attention. She crawled over broken glass—sharp shards of it bit into her knees—but she had to make sure he was all right.

Then, to her amazement, she saw Kirby's little feet dangling against the bottom of his high chair. She felt such relief that she cried out. But as she turned to crawl out from under the table, her cry of relief turned into a scream.

Because there, on the floor behind her, amid the broken glass, lay the body of the giant bird. It was half stuffed into the bag she'd been forced to carry. Its head lolled to one side, limp and nearly lifeless. Its sharp blue eyes, now dull and unblinking, stared at her.

Evie awoke with a jolt. It was that nightmare again, the same one she'd been having since her mother died. Her heart pounded in her chest and she couldn't catch her breath. It seemed that the thick blackness in the room was sucking her up and suffocating her.

She grabbed hold of the bedpost—a life raft in the nightmare of watery darkness around her.

Drenched with sweat, she had to fight the urge to cry out as she'd often done when she was younger. Instead, she opened her eyes wide, praying to see even a sliver of light under her bedroom door.

"One hundred, ninety-nine, ninety-eight, ninety-seven . . ." She counted to herself, just as Gram had taught her. By ninety-six, Evie's heart was beating almost regular again, but she was wide awake.

Godfrey Mighty, it was always the same. That feeling of terror when familiar, friendly things turned bad. That feeling of trying to help and not being able to do it. And the horrible fear of thinking that Kirby had fallen and broken his bottle. Evie bit her lip and pressed her eyes shut tight. She *wouldn't* think about it. Wouldn't think about that time when she was only six, the year her mom died. The year that she'd tried to take care of everybody like a good girl. She pushed the thoughts away.

Damn that dream! It didn't come as often as it used to, but when it did it terrified her just as badly as it had when she was little. It was the last reminder of that awful year, the year before her father went into that hospital and they went to live with Gram. When she was awake she could keep those memories under wraps. But at night—well, keeping them out of her dreams was a problem she hadn't been able to overcome.

She reached over and plugged in the night-light. She knew that just a little bit of light would have warded off the dream. She would make it a point not to forget to plug it in again.

"There's nothing in that dream to be afraid of," Evie told herself for the hundredth time. "Nothing." She flipped over her pillow and punched it hard with her fist before letting her head drop onto it. Evie fought to push the last remnants of the dream aside and finally fell asleep.

❦

The day dawned gray and drizzly. It matched the fuzzy feeling in Evie's head—the exhausted, unsettled feeling she always had the morning after that dream. It was a feeling that she'd missed some small detail that would have made the whole thing make some sense. Every time she'd had the dream, she'd willed it to be the last time. And just when she'd managed to nearly forget about it, it would sneak back, as if to remind her that she was not quite as in control of things as she thought. She stared at the night-light still glowing in the gray morning light and ripped it from the socket. She hated the fact that she needed that light. That she needed it to ward off that stupid dream. But she did.

Evie looked out the window. The fog was so thick that she couldn't see halfway out across the yard. It was as though the clouds floating in over the coast had gotten tangled up in the tops of those spiky pines and, satisfied that escape was impossible, had set up permanent house-keeping there. She could forget about going back to explore the place out on the rocks where that painting had been. It was just too wet and foggy.

Still feeling cranky, Evie rummaged through her dresser drawers for some old jeans and a T-shirt. Since Julia was coming to give her her art lesson today, Evie was apt to get dirty. She was normally neat, but today she yanked her clothes out of the drawer haphazardly until she found what she was looking for. Once dressed, she left the drawers yawning open, spitting articles of clothing this way and that. She'd come back later and tidy up, after her lesson and her chores. But for now it felt good to be a little reckless and angry.

Her art box and brand-new sketch pad scraped and screeched across the wooden floor as she pulled them out from under her bed, as though they were reluctant to come out and cooperate. She could hear Julia breezing in, bustling into the kitchen with her grandmother, along with the sounds of *Sesame Street* drifting from the TV in the sitting room.

Evie headed into the kitchen just as Julia was pulling her supplies out of the beat-up leather case she carried with her each week.

Julia herself was one of the most interesting parts of the art lesson. Gram called Julia a New Age hippie. Evie knew that Julia was too young to have been a real hippie, whatever that was, anyway. But there was something about her just the same, and Evie knew what Gram meant.

Evie watched her slender teacher, relaxed and sure of herself, moving gracefully around the kitchen. Julia tilted her head toward the window to face what little light there was. "Light and shadow," she'd said, at least a hundred times. "That's what an artist sees."

Julia threw her long braid over her shoulder. Her hair was the color of cinnamon sticks. Actually, everything about Julia was sort of spicy—from her dark, musky perfume to her bright woven vests and the huge collection of silver bangles that jingled around her thin wrists. And then there were those boots—black, heavy boots that laced up the front, their long, floppy tongues wagging. On anyone else those boots would look big and clumsy, but not on Julia. They peeked out from under her long, gauzy skirts, which Kirby said made her look like a gypsy. Evie eyed those rugged boots with their rubber soles thick as tire treads. They'd be good for climbing those rocks, all right. They were probably good for scaling up and down a makeshift ladder, too, and for making your way over slimy, wet rock to paint. She stared at her teacher, trying to picture her down in that cave between the rocks, painting. It would be just the kind of thing Julia would get a kick out of. She'd have to figure out a way to find out for sure.

"Evie, doll, you ready for your lesson?" Julia smiled across the kitchen at her.

"Uh-huh." She was ready to draw, that was for sure. Evie set her sketch pad on the table while Gram pulled out her oils, brushes, canvas, and easel. This was their weekly routine—Julia would set something up for them to look at. Evie would sketch and Gram would paint.

Julia was taking out a large piece of cardboard covered in black velvet. She peered around the kitchen, tipping her head this way and that, searching for the day's subject.

"Aha!" she said, picking up the ancient geranium in a clay pot, its woody, twisted stems bursting in scarlet blooms. Julia used the velvet-covered cardboard as a backdrop, propped against the screen of the kitchen window, and set the geranium in front of it. She placed it carefully so that she didn't disturb Gram's collection of elephant figurines that paraded across the windowsill.

"Careful!" said Gram. "You know how I feel about my elephants!"

"Of course I'm careful," Julia said. "I love your elephants almost as much as you do."

Gram's elephants—some glass and ceramic, others carved from wood or cut from stone—supposedly brought good luck. Each and every one of them had its trunk pointing up. "That's the key," Gram always said. "An elephant's trunk should always be pointing up to bring good luck." Evie could see that the cardboard set there on the windowsill was making Gram a little nervous.

Finally, the elephants were forgotten in their caravan behind the cardboard, and Evie, Gram, and Julia settled in. Gram sat for a long time, "learning it with her eyes," while Evie picked up her pencil and put it right to the page.

"Hold it," said Julia, placing her hand over Evie's. "Today, before you start drawing, I want to talk about something new—about something called negative space."

Evie paused, impatient to begin.

"An artist not only learns to use her hands," Julia said, "an artist uses her eyes—to look at the world differently." Evie watched Julia, one eyebrow raised in a question.

"The artist doesn't just see the obvious. An artist also sees and makes use out of what *isn't* there."

Evie waited. She wasn't sure what Julia was driving at. She'd put the geraniums there for her to draw. Now she was telling her not to look at them? To look at what *wasn't* there?

Julia ran her finger down alongside the geranium, tracing its shape against the black velvet backdrop. "Here's what I mean," she said. "The artist not only sees the geranium. The artist sees the shapes the geranium creates."

Evie blinked her eyes and the image of the cat rising out of the stone wall jumped into her head. Julia forged ahead, pointing at the backdrop with the end of her pencil. "See—the edges of the flower break the black background into shapes—shapes that wouldn't be there without the flower in front! The flower takes up space, cutting the black backdrop into negative spaces. I want you to *focus* on the negative spaces. The negative spaces share the same edges as the geranium! Draw the spaces correctly, and your geranium will be perfect too!"

Julia smiled broadly. Evie bit her lip. It reminded her of those optical illusions where you look at a drawing of a vase. If you stare at it long enough, the vase fades away and instead you see the outline of two human heads facing one another. But what was the point? She just wanted to concentrate on the geranium and get it down on paper. She tapped her pencil and rolled her doughy gray art eraser between her thumb and forefinger.

Julia nodded toward the geranium. "To develop the artist's eye, you need to look at what *isn't* there. What others don't see is what gives your art depth and character. Try it."

Try as she might, Evie couldn't seem to focus on the black. It made no sense.

Negative space—what a waste of time! She didn't even like the sound of it. Negative—it sounded like down in the dumps, like the opposite of positive, the opposite of sure of yourself.

She looked at her drawing. There was no way this was going to turn out well. She was bored with it already. And her thoughts kept returning to the painting in the cave. She chewed the end of her pencil, looking from Gram to Julia and back again.

"Julia," said Evie impulsively, "do you like cats?" She watched Julia carefully for some sign of recognition, some hint to show that perhaps she'd been the painter.

Julia continued looking over Gram's shoulder at the artwork on the table.

"A little," said Julia. "I really prefer dogs. For companionship, that is." She pointed to a corner of Gram's canvas. "Why not add some white highlights here?" she asked.

Evie persisted. "So, you're not interested in cats at all?

Even interesting"—she paused, thinking of the cat with one green eye and one blue eye—". . . unusual cats?" she finished.

Julia considered for a moment. "Oh, I didn't say that cats don't interest me. I said I prefer dogs for companionship. Cats are too aloof, too independent."

"So you *are* interested in cats, then," Evie said, watching Julia closely for some clue.

"Cats are fascinating, actually," said Julia. "And mysterious. I've read that the ancient Egyptians worshipped them."

"And believed they had magical powers! They were depicted in ancient Egyptian art throughout the time of the pharaohs."

They all turned toward the deep voice that had jumped into the conversation, uninvited.

"Morning, Professor," said Gram, hopping up. "Let me get you some coffee and muffins. Sit down, sit down. There's plenty of room here."

"Please," he said, smiling slightly, "call me Bill." Evie noticed that although he'd answered Gram, he was smiling at Julia. "Bill McAllister," he said, offering Julia his hand. Julia's bracelets clinked as she reached over and shook hands. Evie looked away, blushing, somehow feeling that she was intruding.

Gram cleared a space for the professor, and Evie pretended to draw, glancing from the geraniums to her paper. But she really watched Julia and the professor (no, she corrected herself, Julia and *Bill*) chat about art. It was hard not to stare at him. His eyes were so blue. And they reminded Evie of someone, although she couldn't quite figure out who.

"Art history," he was saying, "at Staffordshire University. I still do a bit of painting, mostly during the summer, when I'm not teaching."

Evie leaned forward in her chair as Gram served breakfast. So he *was* an artist. The thought sent a small shiver along her spine. Maybe he was *the* artist. The one she was looking for! That was when the plan took shape in her mind. It was so bold and daring that just thinking about it made her palms sweat and her cheeks flush. She looked at the adults guiltily, sensing that somehow they might detect her thoughts. But no, Julia and the professor (*Bill*, she corrected herself again) didn't seem to even remember she was sitting there at all. Thank goodness.

Later, Evie thought, after breakfast when Bill left to do whatever it was he was going to do, she'd go up and change the bed linens. Like she always did for guests. Except, while she was in there . . . she gulped as she thought about it . . . while she was in there she'd look around. She'd look for paints, for pictures or photos, maybe—of that cat. There was sure to be some clue, some small hint there, *if, if* he was the artist. She was exhilarated and terrified at the same time. It felt sort of criminal, but she told herself that it wasn't like *stealing* or anything. It was only *looking*. There were no laws against looking. And wasn't the professor always curious about

48

things? Always asking questions? Nothing wrong with being curious, after all.

Bill was thanking Gram for the breakfast and heading for the door.

"Evie."

She jumped, certain that somehow they'd read her mind.

Julia went on. "How's that sketch coming?"

Evie looked down, sure that if their eyes met, she'd give herself away. She shrugged, staring at the page. "Okay," she said. Gram cleared the dishes and Evie pretended to draw as Julia and Bill said goodbye.

Evie fidgeted through the rest of the lesson, her stomach in knots. Her drawing was the worst she'd ever done. Before she left Julia stared at it and mumbled something about it being a step in the right direction. Some step—a teeny-weeny baby step was what Jemmy would call it. But it couldn't be helped. She'd been preoccupied.

Evie got up and headed around to see Gram's painting. It was a flurry of colors, bright yet soft, all the edges blurred together. Evie stared, unsure of how she felt about it. She preferred art that was more real, more like a photograph. Gram stepped back, a smile on her face.

"So, what do you think?" she asked. Before Evie could answer, she went on. "I know, I know, it's not real enough for you. But it pleases me."

And it *was* beautiful. It was just that it wasn't what was there, straggly as ever, sitting on the windowsill, making negative space or *whatever* it was out of that black velvet.

Evie looked at her own drawing again, tore it from her sketch pad in one furious rip, and crumpled it in a tight ball.

She took aim at the trash can near the back door, threw, and missed. It bounced off the screen with a *ping*. She sighed and headed over to pick it up.

That was when something caught her attention—something peering over the dented metal frame of the screen door—a pair of eyes, one blue, one green. A mismatched set blinking lazily beneath a set of snowy white ears.

As Evie rushed to the door the cat bolted. She stared after the small white cat and noticed that it was not completely white after all. There was a touch—a few small smudges—of blue around its dainty paws. And a dab of green at the tip of its tail. Evie recognized the colors—Winsor & Newton oils, she guessed, cerulean blue and viridian green. She opened the door and stepped out on the stoop to get a better look.

But there was nothing there. No cat. No paint. Just a lot of negative space. And a lot of fog.

She paused for a moment, perplexed. Then she took a deep breath and headed inside, determined to search the professor's room before she lost her nerve.

Chapter 7
Caught!

Evie unlocked the door and left it wide open behind her. She'd strip the bed halfway as quickly as she could and place the pile of clean sheets on the edge of the bed. That way, if anyone came in, it would look as though she was in the middle of the job. She tried not to think too much about what she was about to do. Gram insisted that their guests deserved privacy. Evie told herself that she wouldn't even *touch* anything. She'd just look. That was all.

She began stripping the bed. She found, to her delight, that she'd done this job so often she could do it automatically, without looking. While her hands expertly tucked and pulled the sheets, her eyes devoured the room. There wasn't much to see. The leather bag he'd carried stood squarely in the corner. A few articles of clothing hung in the closet. She could see he was the neat type, the type who hung all the hangers in the closet in the same direction and put all his things away. Shoot! She'd hoped he'd be the kind who scattered his belongings around the room—the type she usually disliked. Sloppy guests made tidying up harder.

The bed was just about changed and her stomach was in knots. All the worry about snooping around, and there was nothing out in the open to see! Evie took a deep breath. Where would a neat person put important things? Her heart began to race as she looked from the dresser drawers to the leather bag and back. Of course—the paints would be in one of the drawers or in that leather bag of his. But how could she . . . she squashed the idea before it took shape completely. Grabbing the stripped sheets, she tossed them in a heap in the hallway. Her eyes were drawn toward the stairs. Nobody was around. She nibbled the inside of her cheek and twirled a strand of hair around her finger. One quick look—that was all it would take.

Her hands shook as she opened the first drawer. As it scraped along the wooden frame of the dresser, the bottom of the drawer squeaked and yelped. She shoved it shut, her heart pounding. She stood perfectly still, listening. But it was quiet. No one had heard. She bit her lip and pulled at the drawer again, this time lifting as she pulled.

She looked in the drawer and shut it quickly. She could feel herself blushing. The only thing in the drawer was underwear. Boxer shorts with small checks and paisley designs. She hadn't really given any thought to finding anything in the drawers except the paint. She would have much preferred not to know what kind of underwear the professor wore. The paints could have been hidden underneath the underwear, but there was *no way* she was going to move it. Besides, he didn't seem the type to mix oil paint with underwear.

Scarcely breathing, she opened the other drawers. Except for several pairs of khaki trousers and some socks, all lined up by color, the drawers were empty.

All that was left was the bag. Evie knew that opening the bag was crossing some kind of line, and as much as she wanted to, she knew she wouldn't do it. She pushed at the bag with her foot. It was heavy. She gave it another small push, and something behind it fell with a thud. Evie looked behind the bag. There was a book—a thick, grayish volume. She turned it over. *The History of Art*, it said, in raised gold letters. She could see that many pages were tabbed with those small yellow sticky notes.

She took one more quick look into the hallway and, seeing nobody, sat down cross-legged on the floor and opened the book.

Evie flipped open to the pages he'd tabbed. The first page she turned to was titled "The Ancient World." The subtitle read: "Magic and Ritual—The Art of Prehistoric Man." There were black-and-white photographs of paintings—bulls and horses and deer. As she read the captions under the pictures, her heart raced. *"Wounded Bison (Cave painting), Altamira, Spain,"* she read. *"Black Bull (Detail of a cave painting), Lascaux, France."*

She tried to make sense of the information on the page. It was all about cave paintings! The ones in the pictures had been done thousands of years ago, by cavemen! She skimmed on, excitedly, across the page. It said that these cave paintings were never done out in the open, where they were easy to see, but in the dark recesses of caves, many only reachable by crawling on hands and knees. The cave paintings in France had been discovered by a boy whose dog had fallen into a hole that led into an underground chamber!

Evie thought about how she'd discovered that cat painting and eagerly read on. The book went on to say that cavemen didn't distinguish between image and reality, that they believed that if they painted these animals, the animals would actually appear, thus guaranteeing a good hunt.

Evie was mesmerized by this information. "Wow," she whispered, scanning the page a second time. She thought about seeing the painting in the cave and then having the cat actually materialize. And now she was sure that the professor knew something about this phenomenon! She was more certain than ever that the bag beside her contained the paint and brushes used to create that cat painting. This book practically proved it! It was possible that he was out there right now, despite the fog, planning another painting. She'd have to get out there and check as soon as the weather improved.

She was so absorbed in the book that she didn't hear the small shuffling sound outside the door until it was too late.

"Enjoying that?"

At the sound of the voice Evie slammed the book shut. She'd been caught! She realized that she'd let out some kind of a yell—really a cross between a gasp and a hoot. She could barely breathe. She dropped the book as if it was poison and flew to her feet.

Evie was relieved to see that it wasn't the blue eyes of the professor she was facing. The person in the doorway backed up a little, obviously surprised by her reaction. He was about her age, maybe a little younger. Straight blackish hair hung in his eyes and he blinked behind thick glasses.

"Jeez," he said, "don't get all bent out of shape! You look like a moose caught in the headlights of a tractor-trailer. I only wanted to know what you were reading."

"Who are you, anyway?" Evie asked sharply. "You don't just go sneaking up on people like that! And I *wasn't* reading!" She knew she was babbling, but she couldn't seem to shut up.

"You were too reading," he said, and to Evie's horror he walked into the room and picked up the book. "*The History of Art?*" he read, flipping through the pages. He brushed the hair out of his eyes, adjusted his glasses and looked at her.

"I *wasn't* reading that book," Evie said, grabbing it from his hand. "It fell while I was cleaning up in here. It belongs to one of our guests, and you have no business touching it." She put the book back behind the bag. God, why was she being so rude? She couldn't seem to stop herself.

The boy looked at her through his long bangs again. "You were *too* reading it," he insisted. "I don't see why you're making such a big deal out of it." He shrugged, obviously finished with the subject. "I'm Michael Elliot," he added. There was no trace of annoyance in his voice. "My family's staying here. Your mother told me you'd be upstairs."

The word "mother" triggered something in Evie— something that felt like having the wind knocked out of her.

"My *mother* told you?" she asked. The tone of her voice was a bit like acid. She wasn't sure whether she felt like crying or rearranging the glasses on this kid's face. He looked at her with a confused expression and pointed toward the stairs.

"The lady downstairs. She told me you were here." He shrugged again and pushed at his floppy hair.

"My mother is dead," said Evie. "That was my grandmother you were talking to."

The boy flinched a little. Part of Evie was glad—it was a kind of a payback for triggering that feeling she got whenever her mother was mentioned. But she knew she was making the boy uncomfortable when he really didn't de-

56

serve it. Had she not been caught snooping in that book, she never would have spoken to him that way. But it was too late to back off.

He stared at her and she stared back. She expected him to drop his eyes, but he didn't. "Sorry," he said. Evie tried to detect sarcasm or anger in his voice, but there was none. It was matter-of-fact, the uncomfortable moment apparently forgotten.

Now she was embarrassed. "Just forget it." She pushed past him and picked up the pile of sheets in the hallway, eager to get away.

"I have work to do," she said, motioning Michael out of the professor's room. She shut the door firmly and felt the boy's eyes following her. Her surprise turned to annoyance as he fell into step beside her. *If he thinks we're going to be friends,* thought Evie, quickening her steps, *he'd better think again.*

And for about the hundredth time she wished that Eliza was home—because if she'd ever needed a friend to talk to, a friend she could trust, she needed one now.

Chapter 8
Spelunking

It was days before the fog lifted. Evie'd been stuck inside all week with the boys—and with that pesky Michael Elliot. Today the sun seemed especially bright, and Evie couldn't wait to get out and enjoy it.

"But you promised!"

Jemmy stuck out his bottom lip and stood with his arms folded. Evie just shrugged and tried to hide the smile that curled around her mouth. From the moment she woke up and saw the sun streaming in her window, she knew that they'd be returning to the rocks—the boys in search of the cat, and Evie in search of . . .

Her heart raced at the thought of the painting, of the

driftwood ladder, and of the cave. She felt a curious mixture of excitement and fear. When the boys had come in, begging, with their backpacks strapped on, canteens from the army-navy store buckled on their belts, she'd stayed cool. She'd wanted to go, for sure, but she knew if she seemed too eager, they'd catch on to her secret and never leave her alone for a minute.

And then there was the problem of Michael. As much as she'd wished for someone her age to spend the summer with, she hadn't wished for someone like him. He was too bold, too curious about things. He had no common sense, always speaking whatever was on his mind, oblivious to what people around him were thinking. He was not one to be sensitive and leave well enough alone. He couldn't even see that he annoyed her. He followed her around worse than her little brothers. She especially didn't want him around today. Not when she had important exploring of her own to do. Michael's mother had said something about doing some antiquing today. With any luck she'd be taking Michael with her.

"So, are we going or not?" asked Kirby impatiently.

"All right," Evie said through a yawn, stretching her arms over her head, "just give me a little time to get ready."

Inside of a half hour they were out the door and on their way. "Be careful," Gram called after them.

Evie shielded her eyes from the sun with one hand and carried her sketchbook in the other. After the long spell of fog and drizzle, the blue sky, without a cloud in sight, seemed so wildly bright that it took a while for her eyes to adjust.

She led the boys far from the spot where she'd slipped—she couldn't risk having either of them getting hurt. They set off to find the cat, and she watched them over her shoulder. She hoped that as she approached the far edge of the rocky cliffs she'd be able to keep an eye on them.

As Evie climbed farther and farther out on the rocks, a voice in her head told her that she should know better, that she should turn back. But that voice was overpowered by a feeling she'd rarely had before—a feeling of reckless excitement.

Evie set her mouth in a determined line, shushed that careful, nagging voice, and let herself be pulled on. She barely thought about retracing the steps she'd traveled the last time. She just let herself be pulled.

She didn't stop until she found herself in the spot where she'd climbed from the cave. The spindly pine ladder reached up toward her, encouraging her, inviting her back.

Nervously, Evie sucked in the side of her cheek and nibbled. Her brothers were barely visible from where she stood—two small dots bobbing along the distant outcropping of stone. She knew better than to let them out of her sight. Still, they were nowhere near the spot where she'd slipped, and they were nowhere near the edge. They were probably looking in the shallow tide pools where the cat, *that* cat, might be dining on minnows or starfish or snails. They'd be busy there for a while, that was for certain.

Reassured by that thought, Evie squatted down and glanced over her shoulder. Her knees felt rubbery and her palms sweaty. The tree hadn't looked as tall when she'd scaled it the last time, the tide at her heels. It was probably because she hadn't had time to think about falling. Drowning had been the bigger concern. But this time, looking down into that pit, the tree seemed more like a giant sequoia than a pine. Evie took a deep breath and eased one foot over the side. She gently dabbed about with her toe, as though she was testing the temperature of too-hot bathwater. She eased her foot down, down, down, until she found a sturdy foothold.

She lowered herself over the side, her sketchbook pressed tightly under her arm, and inched her way down into the pit.

When she finally felt solid rock beneath her feet, she let out her breath in a rush. How long had she been holding her breath, anyway? The thought that she could only hold her breath for about a minute was reassuring—it meant that the boys couldn't have wandered too far.

Evie moved quickly along, squinting into the shadows cast across the narrowing ledges of rock. And then she reached the spot—the spot she was looking for where the sun cut through and bounced off the stone like spun gold.

She wasn't disappointed. She had known all along that she wouldn't be.

The new painting was even more surprising than the

last. At first glance, she saw that it was a crude landscape, a view of Coleman's Cove from the rocks. But the heavy brushstrokes and thick globs of paint—they were nothing at all like the delicate details in the last painting. She stepped up for a better look. As she moved in closer, it was as though she'd turned the knob on a pair of binoculars—the picture seemed to become even *more* out of focus, even more clumsy and blurred.

Instinctively Evie backed up. It was amazing. The more she backed up, the clearer the image became. Back . . . back . . . slowly back. It was like peering into a kaleidoscope, the bright colors shifting, swirling, and changing shape.

Then her heart quickened. The globs of paint suddenly came together in front of her, bringing the painting into sharp focus. The large gray-brown glops became the rocks at Coleman's Cove. The blue and green strokes, the water. And there on the rocks, at the summit, several small, bright strokes had transformed into three small figures. Two smaller figures leading the way, and a taller figure behind them, her long blond hair tossed by the wind. And off to one side, a careless white blob became a small white cat, crouched behind a tousled scrub of brush. Just below the cat the letters were scrawled—C A T. As if to label the white blob.

But wait. Artists don't *label* their paintings. They *sign* them. The image of the cat retreating from the back porch with traces of blue and green smudged on its paws and tail flashed across her mind's eye. Could the cat itself somehow be responsible for these paintings? It was a creepy thought. But Julia and Bill had told her that the Egyptians believed cats had magical powers. And that book of the professor's—it had said something about magic, about the animals from the paintings actually appearing. Maybe the professor *knew* about it. Maybe he was here trying to prove it. To prove that the cat—that magical cat—was creating these images. Or perhaps the professor wanted people to *think* the cat was responsible! He could have set it up to look as though the cat did it. Maybe he was the artist after all.

Either way, whoever the artist was had been watching them! Evie shivered. She took another step back and bumped into something. "Ahh!" she yelled. The wild, animal sound that came out of her mouth startled her and set her hands trembling. She spun around, only to find that what she'd bumped into was just the opposite wall of stone.

Crazy, she thought, this is crazy. There's nothing here to be afraid of. She just had to get back to the boys. Of course—that was why she felt this jumpy. She calmed herself and looked at the painting again. She opened her sketchbook and pulled the pencil from the spiral binding. Her fingers felt big and clumsy, and the pencil felt like a foreign object in her hand.

She studied the painting and willed the pencil to move on the page. She copied the shape of the rocks, the pointy

pines on the horizon. She paused and looked from painting to pad. Godfrey Mighty, her picture was pathetic!
Compared to the painting, it looked stiff and lifeless. Furious at herself, Evie yanked the page from the binding. The
tearing sound echoed off the rocks and startled her.

"Wow! Look at that!"

Evie knew the voice. She spun around. Michael stood
gaping behind her, pushing at his hair and gawking at the
cave painting.

"What are you doing here?" she whispered. It was more
like a hiss. She was too furious to yell. He had invaded
what she'd come to think of as her private space. Michael,
as usual, didn't notice.

"I saw you leaving and I yelled and yelled for you but
you didn't hear me. I figured I'd catch up." He was still
staring at the painting. "Who painted this?" he asked. "It's
awesome."

It would do no good to complain about him following
her. He wouldn't care. And Evie suddenly had the urge to
talk. She had kept quiet about it for so long that the words
just bubbled up toward the surface. But she was not like
Michael, always talking without thinking. And she
couldn't speak as freely with him as she could have with
Eliza. The words she wanted to say just caught in her
throat. And the idea of a magical cat—the idea that
seemed so possible a moment ago felt foolish there on the
tip of her tongue. She'd have to be careful about what she
said.

"I don't know who the artist is," she said. "And no one knows about this place except me. Me and the artist." Even though she couldn't be positive about that, Evie felt sure it was true.

Michael reached out his hand and touched the edge of the painting.

"It's wet," he said.

"And it will be gone when the tide comes in," said Evie.

Michael looked at her. "How do you know?"

She'd already let the cat out of the bag.

"I know because this is not the first painting I've seen here." It felt good to finally say it.

And then, another sound. A clink, like the sound of a penny dropping in a fountain. And a dragging, shuffling noise, coming from that dark place, that cave place, deep within the rocks. Gorry, what in the world was it?

She wasn't waiting around to find out, and apparently Michael was even less eager than she was. He was already rushing back toward the ladder. She dropped the sketch, now wrinkled and damp from her sweaty hands, turned, and ran after him. She held the sketchbook between her teeth as she scaled the pine. She wasn't sure if the metal taste in her mouth came from the cheap tin spiral of the pad or the steely fear that rose up from her gut and filled her mouth. Something frightening was in that cave. Even Michael felt it. She'd never seen anyone move so fast. She climbed up the ladder behind him, wondering whether he'd have the sense to keep quiet about the whole thing.

This time, when she reached the top, Evie didn't look back. She grabbed hold of Michael's arm and stared into his eyes, owlish behind his glasses.

"You will *not* tell anyone about this," she said, narrowing her eyes. "You won't!"

He looked at her seriously, considering. He was huffing and puffing, and she could see small beads of sweat sitting along his upper lip.

"If you tell me everything you know," he said, "I won't say a word."

She looked at him closely, trying to determine if she could trust him. He didn't seem capable of lying. But could he keep a secret? He was always talking without thinking first. But she really had no choice. He knew enough already to spoil things for her.

"Okay," she told him. "I'll tell you. But not here. I'll tell you later. But you have to keep it secret, especially from Kirby and Jemmy."

Michael nodded and they ran back along the span of rock to the spot where she'd left the boys.

"What's your hurry?"

She jumped at the sound of the voice.

The boys looked at her as if she was a lunatic. Kirby scrunched up his forehead. "I *said*, what's your hurry?"

Evie mopped her brow with the back of her hand. "Oh, it's *you*."

"Who'd you think it was?" said Kirby. The truth of the matter was that Evie didn't know who she'd been expecting. Maybe the mystery artist. Evie saw Kirby look at his little brother and twist his finger in small circles around his ear.

Jemmy giggled. "Evie-Jevie is a cuckoo," he said. And in the same breath, "Hi, Michael."

Michael waved—a habit he had even when people were close enough to say hello to.

"We're ready to go," said Kirby. "How about you?"

In answer, Evie and Michael started off toward the grove of pines that separated the inn from the cliffs. The boys ran until they had overtaken them. A chill ran up Evie's spine as she realized that except for Michael, they were in the same position they'd been in, in the painting. She suddenly felt eyes on her, and turned, expecting the cat to dart out from behind one of the stubby, windswept bushes that held on in the thin strips of soil between the rocks. But she didn't see a patch of white or a snowy streak anywhere along their path.

What she saw, off in the distance, was Julia. She could tell by the coppery hair and the billowing skirt. But Julia wasn't alone. She was walking with a tall man. The professor. Bill. Evie was sure of it. Michael noticed too. "What are they doin' coming out here?" he asked. Evie shrugged. But she was thinking . . . maybe they weren't coming—maybe they were leaving. Maybe they'd been painting.

Maybe . . . Evie shook her head. There were just too many questions. She'd tell Michael all about it. Maybe he, in his no-nonsense way, could help figure it all out.

At the inn, Evie waved a hello to Pop and plopped

down on the back steps. Jemmy and Kirby stood facing her.

"Aren't you going inside?" asked Jemmy. Pop nodded toward the boys and winked at Evie and Michael.

"Ayuh," he said under his breath, "those two are up to no good."

Evie looked at her brothers standing stiffly in front of her. Pop, as usual, was right. They were hiding something, that was for sure. Pop raised an eyebrow and went back to sanding the porch railing.

"I'm just going to sit here for a minute," Evie said. Jemmy started to squirm. She pretended to be very interested in peeling back the rubber edge around the toe of her sneaker. Michael stared directly at the boys while Evie watched them closely out of the corner of her eye.

Kirby poked at his brother with his elbow. "Let's go around front," he said. The two of them waved and took several steps backward, falling all over one another. They scrambled to grab the backpack that seemed to be weighing Jemmy down. The backpack took on a life of its own, bulging and wiggling beneath Kirby's hands.

That did it! "Hey," said Evie. "What have you got in there?"

Before they could run, Evie turned Jemmy around and unbuckled the clasps of the backpack. Pop looked over and let out a whistle. "I don't want to be here when your grandmother sees that!"

Evie looked into the backpack and found herself face-to-face, eye-to-eye with the C A T.

That's when the idea struck her. If she could keep the cat, she'd hold the key she needed to unlock the mystery of the paintings. She looked up toward the kitchen window at her grandmother's silhouette and lifted the cat from the backpack.

There *had* to be a way.

Chapter 9
Food for Thought

It had become a nightly ritual—sitting around the low oval mahogany coffee table in the parlor, playing Monopoly, Parcheesi, or sometimes cards. Tonight the Monopoly game began with Evie, Michael, Julia, and Bill. Kirby and Jemmy, who usually begged to be included, were outside, catching fireflies in jelly jars. Mr. Elliot, Michael's father, sat in the wing chair reading his *Boston Globe* and Mrs. Elliot sat out on the porch knitting.

They seemed so old, the Elliots. Not in age, really, but in the way they acted, so serious and polite. Some nights Gram or Pop would join Evie and Michael in a game, but never the Elliots. Evie wondered what it must be like to be Michael, an only child living with two stuffy parents who never got excited or angry or got their hands dirty. No wonder he was peculiar.

Evie rolled and landed on Tennessee Avenue. Only she and Michael were still playing. The Elliots were getting ready to "retire for the evening," as Mr. Elliot put it, and Julia and Bill had wandered into the kitchen, where Gram was dishing out peach shortcake. It seemed that Julia joined them more and more often for dinner these days—and then stayed on into the evening. Julia and Bill had become pretty friendly in the week since he'd arrived, that was for sure. All the more reason to wonder whether they could be working together on those paintings.

The Elliots gathered their things and started up the stairs. "Good night, son," they said. Michael barely nodded their way, but Evie noticed their eyes watching him. No, actually, she noticed their eyes *loving* him. For a second, her insides lurched—she'd often wondered what it would be like to be adored by a pair of living, breathing parents.

Her eyes automatically went to the framed picture on the shelf—an old photograph of her mother and father. They smiled out of the photo, and Evie moved over a bit, positioning herself in what seemed to be their line of vision. She squinted a little, blurring the photograph. That made it easier to pretend that they were looking at her the way Michael's parents looked at him.

Michael followed her gaze.

"Those your parents?" He got up and walked over to the photo.

71

"Uh-huh." She quickly picked up the dice and shook them in her hand. "It's your turn," she said, eager to change the subject.

"So, where's your father, anyway?" he said.

God! Leave it to him to just blurt out a question like that. Sometimes even Jemmy had more sense than Michael did.

"For your information," she said hotly, "my father is sick in the hospital."

She glanced up at him with narrowed eyes, hoping he'd catch on that she didn't want to talk about it. But, as usual, he didn't get it.

"What's wrong with him?"

Evie sighed, an angry, huffing sort of sound. "He's *sick*," she said.

"Well," Michael persisted, "if he's in the hospital, he's *obviously* sick. But exactly what's the matter with him?"

Anyone else would hear her tone of voice and drop the subject. But not him. The truth of the matter was, she didn't know exactly what was wrong with her father. Gram had spoken of nerves and problems with his liver, and that it wasn't the kind of thing you just got better from. He was too sick for visitors most of the time. So they didn't talk about it. They just didn't.

Evie shrugged, unsure of what to say. Michael pressed on.

"How long's he been in the hospital?" he asked.

"Since I was six," said Evie.

"He's been in the hospital for *six years*?" exclaimed Michael. "And you don't know what's wrong with him?"

He just didn't know when to shut up!

Michael continued staring at the photograph.

"You know," he said, "funny thing . . . you know who your father looks like?"

Evie didn't answer. She was busy scooping the game pieces, play money, houses, and hotels and tossing them noisily in the box. Michael didn't seem to notice.

"He looks a little like the professor. Same eyes."

Evie's stomach did a queasy little flip.

"He doesn't look anything like the professor!" She said it with a conviction that she really didn't feel. It wasn't his face or his hair. It was the eyes—sharp and blue. She realized now that the first time she'd set eyes on the professor, those eyes of his had just jumped out at her. At the time she hadn't realized why. Michael, of all people, was right. The professor *did* have her father's eyes. She was embarrassed to have Michael be the one to point it out to her. She should have recognized it herself.

"Hey!" yelled Michael, looking back at the game board. "Why are you cleaning up? We weren't finished yet!"

"I don't want to play anymore," said Evie curtly. She sounded like Jemmy when he got cranky, but she didn't care.

Michael stared at her with that totally blank look that infuriated her. You couldn't even pay him back for his insensitivity by annoying him! He was totally immune.

Evie wondered if it had something to do with those ador-ing parents of his. A feeling that he could do no wrong.

"So," he asked, wiggling his eyebrows dramatically, "are we going to the . . . tomorrow?" He wiggled his eyebrows rather than saying the word "cave" aloud. Jemmy and Kirby could be around listening. You just never knew.

Since she'd told him everything, Evie knew how much he wanted to go back there. But she'd had enough of him for a while. She wanted to go back to the cave herself without him tagging along. He'd edged in on what she'd come to think of as her own private mystery, and she resented it. Just as she resented his endless questions.

She folded the game board in half and shoved it back in the box.

"Maybe," was all she said. She'd decided that she'd rather try to slip out without him.

Michael went upstairs and Evie tiptoed into the kitchen. Gram and Julia and Bill had made their way out to the front porch. She resisted the urge to join them, to look into those blue eyes of his.

Although she'd left Michael behind, the feelings he'd stirred up stayed with her. She was cross and irritated over the fact that his annoying words made sense. It *was* ridic-ulous that she didn't know exactly what was wrong with her own father. It's just that Gram had always made it clear that it was better to leave it alone.

But what if Gram was wrong? Evie was so surprised at the idea that she stopped short. It was as though this new idea suddenly set loose a whole new tidal wave of ideas, none of them very pleasant. Evie twisted a strand of blond hair around her finger and walked quietly into the dining room. What if her father thought they had all forgotten about him? She glanced out the window at her grandmother, on the porch reading Julia and Bill's fortunes. Evie looked away. Gram had a way of just *knowing* things. It was hard to imagine her being wrong about something as important as Evie's own father.

But still the tidal wave of doubt forced an idea to take shape in Evie's mind. Her heart raced as she made her way back into the kitchen. She grabbed her sketch pad and pencil from the counter, tore out a single sheet, and sat down at the table. It was such a simple idea, but the fact that she'd never really considered it before made it seem dangerous and exciting. She knew how to head a letter—just as she'd learned in school.

Dear

She paused and stared at the page. Already a problem. She'd called him Daddy once. She knew that. But it seemed babyish. "Dad" didn't feel right either. You don't, after six years, just write a stranger a letter and begin "Dear Dad."

She chewed the pencil.

Dear Father,

She erased it as soon as she read it. It sounded like a prayer. Jeez, how stupid could she be? She threw the paper away and grabbed another piece. She had to hurry. Gram would be coming in a little while. She began on the new sheet, leaving off the greeting altogether.

I know that it has been a long, long time since you have heard from me. But I am wondering how you are doing.

She thought about asking him what was wrong with him exactly, but it sounded too much like Michael. There were suddenly many things she'd liked to have asked, like Do you ever think about me? Will I ever see you again? Do you even remember us? But she wasn't sure she really wanted to know the answers to those questions.

I am twelve now, Kirby is eight, and Jemmy is six. We found a cat and have been taking good care of it. It is white and has one green eye and one blue eye.

She paused. There was no point in writing if she didn't ask him what she wanted, no, what she *needed* to know. She took a deep breath and plunged forward.

Maybe you can write to me and tell me how you are doing. I really do want to know.
Love

Evie had a weak feeling at the sight of that last word. She erased it carefully and rewrote the closing.

Your daughter,
    Evie Johannson

She read it over once, folded it, and pulled an envelope out of the kitchen drawer. She glanced back outside to be sure Gram was still busy, and went to the counter. With shaking hands she placed her letter in the envelope and sealed it. She shuffled through the stack of mail stuck beside the flour canister until she found it. The envelope from the hospital in New Hampshire where she knew her father was staying. She wrote the address on the front and quickly, before she could change her mind, stuck it between the neatly labeled bills, held together with an elastic band, waiting for Pop to mail in the morning.

Just then she was distracted by a faint scratching sound from outside. In response, she quickly eased open the refrigerator and took out a small bowl of Gram's clam chowder. She opened the back door and placed the bowl on the steps as she'd done every night about this time. She hoped that the cat would get to it before the raccoons did. Or before Gram noticed. There was no sign of the cat now—he was probably hiding, waiting for his dinner.

She was certain that the cat held the key to those paintings. Either the cat would lead her to the artist, or . . . she still toyed with the idea that maybe that peculiar, magical cat had somehow been responsible for the paintings on his own. Until she knew for sure, it was important to keep the cat around.

She closed the door and peered out through the screen

until two feline eyes acknowledged her, caught in the light from the kitchen, glowing in the dark like a pair of burning marbles.

My cat, she thought and shivered. Her thoughts were interrupted by the sound of Gram making her way into the kitchen with the tray of dirty dishes. Not wanting to face her grandmother, Evie slipped up the stairway toward her room and reminded herself that there was no law against writing your own father a letter.

But she felt like she'd broken a law just the same.

Chapter 10
Stampede!

Evie awoke the next morning and recited in her head the letter she'd written. It was a stupid letter. No greeting. A couple of sentences about the cat that had nothing to do with anything. And what if he *did* write back? Gram was sure to find the letter before she did. What had she been thinking, anyway?

She threw on a pair of shorts and a tank top and made her way downstairs. She could still take the letter from the stack of outgoing mail. She'd take it and tear it up. Maybe someday she'd write another letter. One that made sense. She'd have to work on it, though. Think it through. Take her time.

"Morning," said Gram, smiling across the kitchen table. "Let me pour you some coffee."

"Hi," said Evie. Her eyes traveled to the counter, to the canister. To the place where the mail should have been.

"What happened to the letters?" she asked, fighting to keep her voice calm.

"The Elliots were off early to Freeport—going out to L. L. Bean for some shopping. I sent the mail with them. Did you have a letter for Eliza?"

"Uh-huh," said Evie. "It wasn't important." The thought of Michael pawing through those letters—and maybe finding hers—made the whole thing even worse. Gram raised an eyebrow and slid a cup of coffee across the table toward her. Evie wrinkled her nose. "No thanks," she mumbled. She pushed the cup away and walked out the back door. She could feel Gram's penetrating stare. Gram could probably *sense* the letter. Probably knew she was hiding something. Evie straightened herself up and let the screen door slam behind her.

Jemmy and Kirby were huddled on the ground behind the back porch. Kirby pulled a piece of yarn through the dust, slowly, ever so slowly. The cat stayed perfectly still, every muscle poised to pounce. Jemmy clapped his hands and stamped around behind the cat, trying to get its attention. Evie watched the cat—one blue eye, one green—intently watching the yarn, until one paw, like white lightning, shot out and batted the yarn into a small woolly ball. Kirby laughed and pulled the yarn back, and Jemmy let out a hoot of delight. Neither of them knew how mysterious and extraordinary the cat was. They just thought he was fun to play with.

But Evie could see it. Which was why she was wary of the cat—interested in him, but suspicious.

Gram stepped out onto the porch, frowning at the scene in front of her. Her mouth suddenly twisted up in a disgusted little knot.

"What in heaven's name is my elegant chowder doing out on the back steps?"

Evie could feel her face turning red. She'd been so concerned about the letter that she'd forgotten to take in the bowl she'd put out last night. Gram gave the boys a hard look and turned to go inside, the remains of last night's creamy, thick chowder lining the fine china bowl in her hand. Of course, she figured the boys were responsible. Had she seen the cat? Evie wondered. She probably had.

"Evie . . . ," scolded Kirby under his breath. He gave her an impatient look—the same kind of look she usually gave him.

"Sorry," she said. "But weren't you the ones who wanted to keep the cat? I'm not the only one who can feed him, you know!"

"I'll feed him!" yelled Jemmy.

"I don't want any of you kids feeding that little stray!" Gram hollered out the window. "He'll bring nothing but trouble! Now, you chase that cat out of here right this minute!"

Evie glared at the boys. "Can't you two ever keep your mouths shut?" The boys made a feeble effort to shoo the cat away, and Evie went inside. She had chores to do.

Gram was already fumbling in the back of the linen closet. Evie waited patiently for Gram to hand her the clean sheets and pillowcases. Instead, Gram pulled out mothballs.

"They hate that smell," Gram said, shaking her head and wiping her hands on her apron. "I'm going to put these around the back porch to keep that cat off of the steps!"

Evie groaned inwardly and pulled out the bed linens. Now what?

She made her way up to the professor's room and knocked at the door, even though she knew he was out. He had said he was meeting someone at the University of Maine. Julia was going with him. Evie opened the door and went inside.

She expertly stripped the bed, looking around as she did. The room was as neat as a pin. Just like last time. Except for one thing. The leather bag. It was gone. He'd taken it with him! Evie's heart raced. That was where he must have kept the paints! And today he was out—did he have the paints with him? Was he *really* at the University of Maine? Or was he out on the rocks?

Evie rushed to remake the bed and put in a load of whites for Gram. She had to get over to the rocks in a hurry.

Evie slipped out the front door, making certain the boys weren't following. She ran until she was out of sight of the Cozy Cove and walked, huffing and puffing, through the pines and out to the rocks. Her heart pounded, not so much from the exertion and the heat, as from anticipation.

As she got closer to the spot where her pine ladder stood, she slowed down. She had to be careful. She couldn't afford having Bill see her and run off before being discovered.

Finally, she saw the spot. The top of the pine ladder reached just above the gap in the rock. She approached slowly, cautiously. Like a cat, she thought.

She reached the edge and dropped to her knees, ready for her descent. There was a swoosh and a roar below her.

Evie knew what it was before she looked down. It was the tide. High tide. It splashed and gushed into the space between the rocks, swirling and bubbling around the base of the tree. When that tide came in, it came in! In no time at all, the water had rushed halfway up the ladder. If anyone was down there painting, they'd be underwater by now. The thought caused the hair on the back of her neck to prickle, the way it did during a thunderstorm. She gulped and pushed the thought aside. Bill was smart enough to know better than to go down there when the tide was coming in, wasn't he?

Of course he was. He was a professor, after all.

She sat back on the hard stone and sighed. The tide continued to tumble in. It crept up and up, cascading higher and higher, until she could feel the mist on her face. There was nothing else to do but go home.

Back at the inn, Evie sat at the table with her sketchbook while Gram stood by the sink, rinsing off a huge bowl of blueberries. Evie looked at the back door, imagining the cat, and began to sketch, first the shape of his ears, then his small mouth. She went on to the eyes. Gorry, she'd never get it right! The cat looked lopsided and the eyes seemed flat and blank. Maybe it had something to do with that last art lesson of Julia's—that negative space thing. Evie looked toward the window. The black backdrop was still there, set behind the straggly geraniums.

Evie squinted, blurring the edges, trying to see the black spaces around the plants. The more she narrowed her eyes, the blurrier the image became. It was interesting to do, but it didn't help bring anything into focus. She had somehow hoped that it would be like the seascape at the cave—that adjusting things a little would make everything clearer.

All of a sudden the image came crashing in at her. Evie jumped from the chair. The geraniums flew off the windowsill, raining dirt and dried leaves in all directions. Down came the velvet backdrop, and the caravan of elephants—Gram's special elephants—crashed down after them.

The window screen tilted in haphazardly, flapping in and out. And there on the outside sill stood the problem.

The cat stretched lazily and pushed the bottom of the screen in with his paw. He jumped gracefully from the sill to the floor and padded carefully around the broken flowerpot, black potting soil, broken flower stalks, and cracked and broken elephants. It reminded Evie of a story she'd heard in school about Indians driving great herds of stampeding buffalo off a cliff to their deaths.

"Oh my God! My beautiful elephants!" Evie had forgotten that Gram was even in the room until that moment. The disappointment in her grandmother's voice made Evie cringe. The cat was rubbing up around Gram's ankles, purring. He didn't even notice what a mess he'd made.

Gorry, what would happen now? Evie covered her mouth with her hand and held her breath.

"What was all that noise?" yelled Kirby.

Evie and Gram turned in the direction of the boys, now staring wide-eyed at the scene in the kitchen.

"That's it!" yelled Gram. "The cat goes!"

She swept him up in her hands and held him out in front of her like a bag of week-old garbage.

"You take it all the way back to those rocks where you found it. If I see it around here again, Godfrey Mighty, I swear, I'll call the animal control to come pick it up!"

"But . . . ," blubbered Jemmy.

Kirby shushed his brother. None of them had ever seen Gram so mad. Unlike the boys, Evie was smart enough to sense the hurt beneath Gram's anger. And she felt that in part it was their fault. She knew she should say something, apologize, maybe, but the intensity of Gram's anger kept her quiet.

Gram shoved the cat at Evie. His body felt warm in her arms and she could feel his little heart beating against her chest. She stroked his soft throat and felt him sort of rumbling—a quiet, inside-out kind of purr.

Evie saw Gram kneel down to save what was left of her elephants and found she had to look away. She knew that for the first time in as long as she could remember, she was going to disobey her grandmother. Was this cat worth it? And would she risk losing Gram's trust to keep him?

She gave her brothers a look, then stepped out the door and down the steps. She wrinkled her nose at the mothball smell. The cat looked up at her, wiggled his own pink nose, and sneezed. Without a word the boys followed Evie.

Another look passed between them. Evie felt her face flush warm, and a rush of feeling grabbed at her insides. At that moment she felt closer to her brothers than she'd ever felt before. It was too bad though, that it grew out of their unspoken agreement to disobey Gram. It had always been her and Gram, and Kirby and Jemmy. She was usually in charge of them or looking after them. Now she felt one with them. But it was a feeling she couldn't completely enjoy. She felt like a traitor—a traitor to her grandmother. First by sending off that letter behind her back, and now this. But, traitorous or not, it had to be done. Maybe that was why none of them spoke. Evie guessed they were all a little ashamed.

As they followed Evie down the path, she knew for certain that this was *their* cat. And that they had to find a way, some way, to keep him.

Chapter 11
Shelter

Pop piled several grayish lobster pots beside the shed. Each one was missing a narrow wooden slat or two. Pop eyed the traps carefully, determining how much wood he'd need to make the repairs.

"Lobster tonight," he said as Evie and the boys approached. "Just came back from hauling these in—caught five or six two-pounders."

Pop took out the small motorboat twice a week during the summer to haul in their traps. He'd leave before they got up, usually as early as six. That was when it occurred to her.

"What time did you leave this morning?" she asked.

Pop raised an eyebrow at the sight of the cat, now in Jemmy's arms.

"Usual time," he said, barely moving his mouth.

"Did you see anybody around this morning?" Evie asked. Now Pop raised an eyebrow her way. Evie realized it must have sounded like a peculiar question.

The lie that fell from her lips was surprisingly smooth. "I mean, I thought I heard the professor going out early."

"Ayuh," said Pop, "he and your artist teacher were over to the rocks, walking about. Six fifteen, it must have been."

Evie's heart raced. "I thought he was going out to the University of Maine," she said.

"Don't know about that," said Pop.

So he *had* been out on the rocks. But had he been painting? Had he been there when the tide came in? Again, she pushed the thought aside. He was just too smart to let that happen, even if he was from away. Julia knew the tides and this shore like the back of her hand. She wouldn't stand by and watch the tide roll in over the two of them.

Kirby made an impatient huffing sound. "Come *on*, Evie," he urged. "Let's go!"

Pop glanced at the cat again. "You kids are planning some mischief where that cat's concerned. I say just keep it away from your grandmother."

Evie nodded and pushed open the door to the shed.

The light from outside filtered in, and an army of dust particles floated aimlessly past. It was real stuffy in there. The small, damp shed seemed to hold in a mix of smells—fertilizer, gasoline for the mower, and the deep, musty scent of earth that never saw the light of day.

Gorry, it was hot. Sweat trickled down Evie's back. She wasn't sure whether the heaviness in her arms and legs came from her sorry feelings about Gram and the cat or from the thick humidity. She felt like a garden slug—wet, slimy, and slow. She pushed her hair behind her ears and lifted the sweaty, straggly ends off of her neck. Hot or not, it was time to do what they'd come for.

"How about this?" Kirby held up a wooden crate. It had the words BOOTHBAY FISHERY on the side. Evie looked it over. It probably had been used to pack herring or shrimp. Good. The cat might like the smell of it. The size was about right too, and it seemed sturdy enough. She poked at the small whitish spider eggs hanging in its corners like miniature golf balls. She absentmindedly squashed one between her fingers and the egg burst, sending out hundreds of minuscule baby spiders. They poured over the box like a microscopic army. She threw the box down in disgust and pounded it with her foot. Spiders gave her the creeps, especially since Gram's fortune about making webs, and new spins on old tales.

Satisfied that the next generation of spiders had dispersed, she picked up the box again. "Okay," she said, clearing away the dusty webs, "now we need something to line it with."

Kirby came up with a couple of burlap feed sacks. They felt scratchy and rough, and Evie wrinkled her nose.

"They're kind of stiff and prickly." She pointed over toward the tool bench. "Let's look over here." There was a large box wedged underneath. Kirby ran right over. "Grab an end," he said, "and we'll pull it out."

She and Kirby pulled. The cardboard, spongy and moist, slumped in the humid air and slid easily from under the bench.

Kirby lunged for the lid as though they'd uncovered a treasure chest.

Maybe they shouldn't go through the box. Someone— probably Gram—had gone to the trouble of hiding it under the bench there. Evie's heart began to beat a little faster. "Wait," she said.

Jemmy interrupted. "It's too hot in here!" He was whining and the cat was squirming in his arms.

"All right," she said, "open it."

Kirby threw back the lid and sat back on his heels. There were rags in there—mostly rags and old clothes. Kirby dug around between the cloth. "Look at this . . ."

Evie stared. She felt like swallowing, but her throat was suddenly dry. "I think you should close that box," she said. The words felt thick and cottony in her mouth.

"What is it?" Jemmy inched closer, squinting in the dark.

"Gram wouldn't want us poking around in there, Kirby. I think you should *shut the box*." Her voice had become shrill. She took a deep breath and looked at the small photograph in Kirby's hands.

"It's our mother and father," said Kirby, "with a little girl. . . ." He looked at Evie, fascinated. "I think it's *you,* Evie! And look, there's a birdcage with a little bird. Do *you* remember this?"

The heat in the shed suddenly was too much for her, and she couldn't seem to move. She couldn't tear her eyes away from the photo. Even with the small drops of condensation under the glass and around the frame, she recognized them. There they sat, the three of them, at the table—at *that* table, the one with the eagle's feet clutching the round glass balls. And in a fancy cage behind them was a small bird. The photograph was too old and blurred for her to make out the bird clearly. But Evie knew, she knew as well as she knew her own name, that it was the bird in her nightmare. The bird that mutated and turned bad and carried her off.

Evie shut her eyes tight. There it was, proof that she had had two parents who had once held her, loved her, and posed for pictures with her. She couldn't even remember, yet there she was, smiling between them. And proof that something about that nightmare had some basis in reality. The dream bird actually *had* existed.

Of course, that was why Gram stashed the pictures away, out of sight, where they wouldn't remind you of things, wouldn't make you ask questions.

Kirby studied the picture closely and moved to place it

back in the box. Jemmy plopped the cat on the ground and grabbed the photograph from Kirby.

"I wish I had a mommy and daddy to take a picture with," he said, staring at the photograph. There wasn't any real sadness in his voice. He sounded like other kids who wish for a pony or a built-in swimming pool. Kids who know it must be nice to have those things, but never really expect to have them.

Evie yanked the photo from Jemmy and slammed it back into the box.

"We're in a hurry, and there's no time for goofing around." She jammed the box back under the tool bench and stood up.

"But I wanted to see that picture of my mommy and daddy!" Jemmy's mouth was set in a stubborn line. Great. Any minute he'd be wailing.

"Do you want us to lose this cat *for good*?" She was shouting now. She knew she shouldn't, but she couldn't help it.

Jemmy stared at her.

"If we don't go take care of this *right now*, you can forget *ever* seeing this cat again. *Ever!*"

Jemmy sniveled, scooped up the cat, and hugged it tighter. Kirby was staring at her as if she was crazy. That made her even more mad. Her anger seemed to lighten the heaviness in her arms and legs. With one quick move she grabbed the feed sacks and crate from the floor and pointed toward the door. The boys paused.

"Go!" she yelled. Kirby threw her a disgusted look as the two of them trudged out the door.

Evie stepped back into the shadows, slid her hand into the box, and felt around for the photograph. Something else was shoved in there between the old clothes folded neatly in the box. Evie's heart pounded. She grasped and pulled.

Tubes of paint. Used-up, mostly. The same kind Pop had dragged out of the shed the day after the storm.

Kirby stuck his head back inside.

"Are you coming or what?"

"I'll be right there!" said Evie. "Just go! I'll catch up!"

She stuck her hand back in the box until she found the photograph. She slipped it into her pocket, ran to catch up with the boys, and led them along the path out toward the rocks.

Chapter 12
Encounter!

The sun was sweltering out there on the rocks. Evie half expected the water left behind in the tide pools to boil in the heat. She began to itch all over at the sight of the small swarms of no-see-ums flitting over the stagnant water. She was tempted to stop and scratch last week's minge bites on her ankles, but she resisted the urge.

"Here's a good spot!" Kirby had run ahead and stood perched across two large boulders. "We could jam the box right in here," he said, "in between the rocks."

Evie shook her head. You couldn't put the box right out here in the sun. The cat would die of the heat. And besides, it was too obvious. She knew a better place, a sheltered, out-of-the-way place. The place where the pine ladder led down into the cave.

But how could she keep the boys away? She stopped and nibbled the inside of her cheek.

"Listen," she said, "I think we might need a lookout. Gram or Pop might suspect that we're up to something and come out here to see."

The idea of being a lookout obviously appealed to Jemmy. He perked up a little and handed the cat to Kirby. "I'll watch for them," he said.

Kirby narrowed his eyes a little and looked at Evie. He was suspicious, she could tell. It would be important not to seem too pushy.

"I guess Jemmy *would* make the best lookout," she said. Kirby's eyebrows shot up and Evie waited.

"I don't think so," said Kirby. "We'll *both* watch for them."

Jemmy's face fell and Evie had to remind herself not to react. It had been easier than she'd thought.

"Are you sure you can handle it?" She looked at them closely.

Kirby sighed. "Of *course* we can handle it! We'll watch until you set up the box. Then you can watch and we'll go see where you put it."

"Okay, but be careful."

She took the cat and put him in the box. He seemed to like it just fine, rolling over onto his back and rubbing himself on the burlap.

"Goodbye, Robinson," said Jemmy. "We'll bring you some food tomorrow."

Robinson? The name didn't seem to fit, but Evie wasn't

going to argue. She set off in the direction of the cave, imagining the spot where the box would fit, circling around farther back than she needed to, just in case the boys decided to follow. Their plan, if you could call it that, was to fix the cat a cozy place to stay and bring food for him every day. As she made her way along she worried. The cat was smart enough to find his way back to the house, and then who knew what Gram might do? How could they be sure he would stay near the box? And even if he did stay, what would happen in the winter? And besides all that, the boys would insist on coming to see where she put the box, and that would be dangerous. The whole thing was stupid, she realized, a babyish, stupid plan that would never work.

Sweat trickled down her back and the edges of the burlap scratched at her bare arms. Suddenly the cat sat up, his whiskers twitching. Before Evie could think twice the cat jumped from the box and began running over toward the pines that fringed the rocky area to which they were headed.

Shoot! Evie dropped the crate and ran after him. "Robinson! Here, kitty," she called. She whistled softly and made small kissing sounds. But the cat didn't even prick up an ear. He continued on his way, oblivious to her. Something about that independence infuriated Evie. She scrambled after him, between the trees and into the shade. "Robinson! Come back!" she yelled. But she was talking to herself.

In her determination to keep her eyes on the flash of white skirting through the woods, Evie didn't see the crude structure until she was upon it. If it hadn't been for the cat stopping and rubbing himself against the crooked pine branch holding up the entranceway, she might have run on past it.

It was a lean-to, held up with peeling pine branches. It was set against a steep incline, its back wall solid stone. Its walls were constructed with smaller branches, and sheets of cardboard and scrap wood made the roof. It looked as though it had been built long ago—maybe as a clubhouse. Evie's heart raced. It would be perfect! A little house in the woods for their cat! They could come out here and feed him. They could even fix it up, set it up like a secret hideout.

The cat meowed and disappeared inside. Evie followed him. It was dark in the lean-to, and at least a few degrees cooler. It took a moment for her eyes to adjust to the dark. The cat rubbed around her ankles and she knelt down and stroked his soft fur. It was as though he'd led her here, as though he already knew this place. And maybe he did.

Evie looked around and sniffed. There was a familiar smell, familiar but somehow out of place. Her eyes widened at the realization. Linseed oil. That was it! Linseed oil and oil paint. She jumped to her feet and began to look around.

In one corner was a small plastic milk crate lined with cardboard. She dug beneath the rags on top and felt them—tubes of paint, and brushes. She squinted in the darkness and lifted one of the rags. Her heart pounded. She stared at it, trying to place what it was about the rag that looked familiar.

Then she knew. Beneath the smudges of paint she could make out the pattern of the cloth. It was red with small blue flowers. She saw it all of a sudden—her grandmother's apron, the one with the huge pockets that she'd worn until the edges frayed and went too stringy to mend. And there were others. One rag had been an old bathrobe, the pale yellow plaid that Gram had worn every summer until she got a new one last Christmas.

So Gram had been using this place, this little hut in the woods, as a place to come to and plan those cave paintings! But when? And why?

Evie thought she heard a scuffling sound outside. Shoot! She couldn't believe that they'd left their post and followed her! She stuck her head out the doorway but didn't see them. Well, this spot was just too good to keep secret, anyway. But what about Gram? Wouldn't she find the cat out here when she came to paint?

It had gone on long enough. Evie would confront her grandmother today. As soon as they were alone. She knelt once more to stroke the cat, so white against the brown earth floor of the lean-to. A ray of sunlight shone on him, illuminating his snowy coat. Slowly, a shadow crossed the sunlight. Tall, dark, humanlike.

Evie stood, hugging the cat in her arms, and turned around.

She gasped. She was standing face-to-face with a madman. She stared at him, unable to move.

He was hunched and thin, and his clothes, faded and colorless, flapped about him like the rags on a scarecrow. He had the copper-colored, sun-scorched skin of a fisherman, but it hung around his skull in wrinkled folds, as though whatever was once inside of him had shriveled up and shrunk down to nothing at all. His bright blue, watery eyes stood out of his sunken face like the turquoise sky over a desert. But despite their brilliant color, those eyes were dead. Dead, blank, and unseeing, that lunatic stare of his held Evie in her spot like a barnacle fixed to a rock. There was nothing behind those vacant eyes, nothing human to connect with. Godfrey Mighty, where had she seen that look before?

He reached out toward her, his dirty hand and grimy fingernails moving in a dazed way. Closer and closer. She watched, horrified. She stepped to the side, but he blocked the doorway.

One thin, surprisingly strong hand locked around her wrist, the pointy fingers pressing into her skin.

"No!" she screamed. "No!"

Chapter 13

Repercussions

With every ounce of strength she had, Evie wrenched her wrist out of his dry, papery grasp. He stared at her, his mouth hanging slightly open, his face expressionless. With an animal kind of grunt and her eye on the doorway, Evie flung the cat full-force at the madman in front of her. He stumbled to the side, and Evie used that moment to crash past him. He toppled over and she ran. It was a blind, furious, and mindless kind of running. Her feet pounded and her chest heaved. She only knew that she *had* to get away from those eyes.

She finally reached the rocks, and she was grateful for the scorching sunlight. But she didn't stop. Not yet. She couldn't stop until she was out in the open, out where he couldn't grab her again. Finally, exhausted, she sat, facing the direction from which she'd come so that he couldn't sneak up on her.

She slumped over and tried to slow her racing heart and think clearly. She couldn't get the madman's face out of her mind. The image sent her to her feet. She had to get the boys home. She had to keep them away from that spot. And she had to confront her grandmother.

But it was the feeling, the *overpowering* feeling, that she'd had this experience before that truly terrified her. She could almost taste the fear, and she felt it nipping at her heels as she flew over the rocks.

"Evie, what *took* you?"

Kirby and Jemmy rushed toward her.

"Tell us where you put the box." The two of them started off in the direction from which she'd come.

"Wait!" said Evie. She paused, trying to think of exactly what she should tell them.

"The cat got away from me." That was true, anyway.

"What do you mean he got away? Where did he go?"

Kirby was looking at her incredulously. Jemmy stuck out his bottom lip and looked from Evie to Kirby and back.

"I was just walking along with him in the box, and it was like something out there scared him. He just sat up and jumped out of the box!" She realized as she said it that it was true. It was as though he'd been frightened. Perhaps he'd sensed the madman before he'd appeared. Another thought struck her. Maybe the madman had been *watching* them. Maybe he'd followed them to the lean-to. Maybe the lean-to was his house. Maybe he lived out there. The thought sent a chill up her spine.

"Well," said Jemmy, "if the cat just ran off, we should go find him."

"Or," added Kirby, "we could just go back to where you left the box and leave some food there. That way he'll find it." He took Jemmy by the arm and turned again to go.

"Wait!" said Evie. "Don't go out there!" They stopped. "Why not?"

Evie gulped. "I saw someone out there. A stranger. Someone I've never seen before. He was creepy. I think there was something the matter with him."

"He was sick?" asked Kirby, confused.

"Well," said Evie, choosing her words as carefully as she could, "not sick like you mean. He was, well . . . weird, crazy maybe. Like he didn't really know what was going on. He was scary, and I think we should make sure to stay away from him. Just to be on the safe side." She added the last sentence as she saw the hint of alarm in Jemmy's eyes.

"But what about Robinson?" Jemmy asked in a shaky voice.

"The cat will make his way back to the inn when he gets hungry," Evie answered, realizing as she spoke that it was true.

Kirby let out an exasperated sigh. "That's why we were going to set up the box for him in the first place. So that the cat *wouldn't* hang around the inn! Gram said—"

103

"I know," Evie interrupted, "but what do you want me to do? The cat got away and there's a stranger out there. I know Gram wouldn't want us out there with a stranger around."

Kirby narrowed his eyes. "There are plenty of strangers around. They're called summer people. You've never been afraid of them before."

Evie closed her eyes for a second, seeing the blank, openmouthed stare of the madman. He was no summer person, that was for sure. Not some tourist out on a nature walk or some professor running around the rocks after her art teacher. No, this stranger was not like that.

"He *wasn't* a summer person. And we're not going back out there. We're going home, *now,* and we'll wait until the cat comes back. Then we'll figure something out." She made sure that her voice had that edge to it that she used when she meant business. Kirby stomped off ahead of her, dragging Jemmy along whining.

Pop was still puttering around the shed when Evie returned.

"I see you got rid of the little pest, eh?" asked Pop.

Evie sat down on the ground beside him.

"You're looking down in the mouth," he said. "What's troubling you?"

Evie thought for a moment. Pop was closemouthed. He could be trusted.

"I was out on the rocks," she said. "Way out, on the other side. And I saw somebody out there."

"Not surprised," Pop answered.

"No," said Evie. "A sort of crazy man. He wore raggy old clothes, and he looked kind of, well . . . crazy."

Pop looked at her sharply. "Did he bother you?"

Evie swallowed. Why was it so hard to say some things? "Well, no," she said slowly, "he just scared me a little."

Pop grunted. "Must have been a vagrant, that's all. Some fellow out of work making his way up the coast. Maybe from Bangor or Bath. Probably harmless. But you ought to stay away from anybody like that. Just to be on the safe side."

Evie nodded. "I'll be careful." She could feel his eyes on her, searching to see if she was telling him everything. She looked down and drew in the dusty ground with her finger.

"Just don't tell Gram, okay?" She looked at him squarely then. "She might keep us off the rocks and that would spoil the whole summer."

"Don't know if I ought to do that," Pop said.

Shoot. She'd never expected him to tattle. Now what?

"Look," she argued, "I won't go anywhere near that side anymore. I'll stay way out in the open, not back in the woods. And I'll see that the boys do the same. And you're right. He was just probably passing through anyway. He's probably already gone on to the next town."

Pop moved his head slightly. You couldn't actually say it was a nod.

That night Evie found herself tossing and turning in bed. Bill still hadn't come back from the university. She kept thinking about the tide rushing in between the rocks.

105

And that letter she'd written—she kept picturing it on its way to her father. Then there were Michael's dark eyes, wide open behind his glasses as she told him the story of the lean-to, of Gram's paint-stained rags, and of the mad-man. (Vagrant, she corrected, he was only a vagrant.) She could feel the knot in her gut all over again, just as she had each time she'd opened her mouth to talk to Gram, the words catching in her throat. She'd never accom-plished it in the end.

So many things she wanted to say, and somehow she was never able to say them. Between all of that and the memory of the madman's face, the feel of his papery hands pressing into her wrist, she could barely close her eyes. Finally, after replaying all of it over and over until it jumbled and blurred together crazily, she slept.

The small bird called her name.

"Evie, Evie."

It was that same voice, deep and familiar. Oh God, that bag she was dragging was weighing her down. She dragged it along the linoleum. It would barely budge. She started to cry. It was too heavy. Way too heavy.

"Mommy!"

No answer. Of course not. Mommy was dead.

The light faded. The walls closed in. The walls were differ-ent this time. Crude pine boughs held them up. They tipped in, closer, closer. A shadow loomed across the ground before her. She dropped the bag and grabbed the cat. The white cat. She carried him with her in the suffocating darkness. She had to take care of him, too.

The cat sprang suddenly from her arms and pounced at the bird. The bird that had spoken to her.

"No," she warned the cat, "stay away from that. . . ." But it was too late. The bird began to grow and grasped the cat in its talons. It swooped, then hurled the cat toward her. The cat's mismatched eyes dilated in terror, and its legs sprawled and thrashed at the air in front of her. She shielded her face from the cat's sharp claws and crouched before the bird, but it was no use. There was nothing she could do. It was out of her control.

The marble-eyed creature lifted her in its sharp talons. Again, it mutated, transformed—growing, bending, and hardening into the wood of the table.

She cowered below the table. The screaming began, and she knew all over again that her brother had fallen. The white cat, calm once again, was rubbing his back along the bottom of the high chair. Kirby's feet dangled there, right where they should be.

The cat suddenly arched his back, pushed back his ears, and hissed. She could see his small, pointy white teeth, bared in a snarl. Her eyes followed to where the cat was staring. And there behind her on the floor was the giant bird, stuffed half in the bag, limp and lifeless.

"Daddy!"

Evie sat bolt upright in bed, awakened by the sound of her own voice. Her heart was racing. She counted backward, "One hundred, ninety-nine, ninety-eight, ninety-seven . . ."

It wasn't working. The panic was more intense than

usual. And the dream, *that* dream, had changed. The cat was now a part of the dream. It was an omen, Evie was sure. A warning.

She suddenly hoped, sincerely hoped, that she'd seen the last of that cat. The last of the cat and of everything else in that nightmare that terrified her.

She lay awake the rest of the night.

Just after the sun came up, she saw Bill drive his beat-up, broken-down car into the driveway. The relief that she experienced (he hadn't drowned after all!) relaxed her enough for sleep to creep up and grab her, unsuspecting.

But she didn't sleep for long. There was a knock on her door and a voice calling her. Michael's voice.

"Get up, Evie. The cat came back!"

Chapter 14
Journeys

There was no time for breakfast. Evie threw on her clothes and followed Michael out to the shed.

"I found him outside the back door, begging for something to eat," said Michael. He peeled back the lid of a small plastic margarine tub. The unmistakable aroma of Gram's chowder burst out. The cat meowed loudly.

Evie grabbed the container from Michael's hand, sloshing a glop of thick chowder onto the floor of the shed. The cat pounced on it and hungrily lapped it up.

"What are you doing?" Michael demanded. "You almost spilled the whole thing."

Evie's mouth was set in a stubborn line. "We are *not*

keeping the cat," she said. "It's caused too much trouble already."

The cat meowed pitifully and rubbed against her leg. She was pulled between an urge to pick him up and hug him or shove him aside with her foot.

Michael looked at her steadily. "Now you sound just like your grandmother," he said. "Don't you ever think for yourself?"

She might have been persuaded to at least give the cat a meal or two, but Michael's words infuriated her. She grabbed the cat up in her arms and bounded out of the shed. She'd show Michael all about thinking for herself. She started off across the lawn and out toward the rocks.

"Evie! Evie, wait!"

A small part of her was relieved that he was close behind. After all, if the madman was still out there, he posed less of a threat to the two of them together. But she would have dearly loved to leave him behind.

She walked quickly across the rocks, glancing back and forth as she went. Michael scrambled behind her, much less agile on the rocks than she was. He balanced the margarine tub in his hand, desperately trying to keep up with her without spilling the chowder. Good, let him struggle. Her head ached with the effort it took to fine-tune her ears and eyes to pick up any motion or sound that didn't belong out there. She strained against the sound of the waves and squinted into the sun that glinted off the bits of quartz and mica in the rocks. She quickened her steps a bit. The cat blinked up at her and adjusted himself in her arms. He seemed to trust her completely, which made Evie feel even worse about carrying him off and leaving him out there. But that was what she intended to do.

Finally Michael caught up to her, huffing and puffing. His words came out in breathy wisps.

"You said yourself that the cat was the key! You chicken out of asking your grandmother to explain what's going on, and then you take the cat, the *key* to the whole thing, and get rid of him!" Michael was red in the face and actually angry. Evie felt a real satisfaction in the fact that she was getting to him. If only his words hadn't struck a note of truth.

"When are you gonna figure things out for yourself instead of just pretending nothing matters? Chasing away the cat isn't going to get you any answers!"

That did it. She whirled around to face him.

"Fine," she said. "Do you have a better idea?"

He looked at her, more calmly now. "Take me to the lean-to," he said. "Take me there and we'll look around until we figure this whole thing out."

Evie stared at him for a moment. She *did* want to figure things out. She really did. And he wanted to help. She shrugged and continued in a huge arc out toward the place where the lean-to stood. For once Michael seemed to understand that she didn't want to talk. She climbed the summit to the place where the trees overtook the rocks and he followed in silence.

At the lean-to she paused. Her heart was pounding and her palms were sweaty. What if the madman was inside?

She motioned toward the door with a sideways nod of her head. Michael walked slowly toward the door and peeked inside. Evie held her breath.

"There's no one here," he whispered. He motioned for her to follow him in, but she shook her head. She'd stay outside and keep watch. She didn't want the madman to sneak up on her like he did the last time and trap them inside.

She knelt in the doorway and dropped the cat to the ground. Michael placed the small plastic bowl on the ground and gave it a stir with his finger. The smell of the chowder wafted up and filled Evie's nostrils. The cat smelled it too and in his eagerness practically toppled it. She gently shoved the cat and the bowl inside the lean-to.

There was a snapping sound off in the distance, like the sound of a twig cracking underfoot.

"Michael!" Evie could barely get the words out. "Michael!"

He stuck his owlish head out the door.

"What?"

"Shhh!" she whispered. "I thought I heard something!"

Michael stepped out of the lean-to. Another snap and a rustling sound. Evie thought she detected a faint movement off deeper in the woods.

"Let's go!" she whispered again. She grabbed him by the arm and they took off back the way they had come.

She only looked back once as she ran. All she saw was the cat's white tail flicking back and forth behind the soft curve of his back. He never even looked up from the bowl as they hurried away. Their feet pounded over the layers of pine needles. Evie listened to the quick, gentle thudding sound and concentrated on keeping a steady pace.

Back on the rocks they paused, huffing and puffing. She looked over her shoulder to see if the cat was following. There was no trace of white anywhere. Or of the madman. They sat down in the sunshine to catch their breath.

"Well," Evie said, gasping for air, "did you see the rags and the paint and stuff in there?"

Michael shook his head. "It was empty. Completely empty."

He was still winded, and paused for a second. "No paint, no rags, no brushes, nothing."

Evie looked at him incredulously.

"But yesterday . . ."

"Well, either your grandmother or the madman cleaned the place out." He paused again. "Unless . . ." His eyes suddenly opened wide behind his glasses. He leaned toward Evie, excited. "Unless the madman was the artist right along. You found his secret den and so he took his paints and stuff and moved on."

Evie looked at him sharply. It did make sense, except for one thing. How could someone so obviously out of it be so talented?

"I don't know," said Evie. "I told you, he was *crazy*."

Michael shrugged. "So was Vincent van Gogh."

Evie raised an eyebrow. "Vincent van Gogh? What about him?"

"He cut off his own ear," Michael explained. "He was crazy. But that didn't mean he couldn't paint."

"But what about the rags? I know they were Gram's."

"I don't know," said Michael. "Maybe he and your grandmother worked together."

That was the dumbest thing Evie'd ever heard! Her grandmother painting with the madman? She rolled her eyes and shook her head. Impossible.

"I noticed that your grandmother was out early this morning," said Michael. "Do you know where she was going?"

Evie shook her head.

"Do you think . . . ," Michael began.

Evie knew what he was going to ask. Had she been painting? There was only one way to find out.

"Come on," she said, and she led the way back to the pine ladder.

When they got there they climbed down without so much as a second's hesitation. They felt their way along the cave walls until they came to the place. Evie's hands grew sweaty as they got closer. She squinted as her eyes adjusted to the dark.

Was the wall blank? She felt a rush of disappointment. She moved closer and turned a bit to the left. Michael edged along beside her.

Wait. She scanned back a little, her eyes devouring the rough walls of the cave as hungrily as that cat had slurped Gram's chowder.

It was as though her brain sensed it ahead of her eyes.

Her heart started thumping even before she recognized the image on the far wall.

She inhaled sharply and her hand flew up to cover her gaping mouth. Michael must have noticed it at the same time. She could hear him gasp beside her.

Staring back at them was a new painting—a portrait of Evie herself! Evie stood looking at the image of her flailing arms, of the white cat sprawling, his paws swimming in midair. She couldn't pull her eyes away from the painting. It was like looking at a twin—a terrified, howling twin. The artist had captured the terror in her wide open eyes, and the whole image seemed almost electric in its sense of fear and urgency. There was so much energy in the painting that Evie half expected the image to turn and run as she had done in real life. And it was labeled, just like all the others—C A T.

That's when she understood. The realization hit her like one of those waves outside crashing over the rocks. All at once she knew for sure who the artist was. The only person capable of capturing her image like that was the madman himself! He'd been the only one who had seen her out there with the cat.

The next realization she had was that he hadn't been a vagrant at all, or just some bum passing through. He'd been around here since she saw that first painting. Maybe he was here right now, watching them. Her skin crawled with goose bumps.

"You were right," she whispered to Michael. "It was him all along." She turned and looked at Michael, who

115

was still staring at the painting. A clinking sound and a shuffling sound interrupted them.

They ran, slipping along the slimy stone floor of the cave, away from the image and the noises coming out of the darkness. They were back at the top of the ladder so quickly that later Evie had almost no recollection of climbing back up. They ran practically the whole rest of the way back home and hauled themselves up the path, breathless and winded.

"I'm glad you're back."

Evie looked up, surprised, at the peculiar tone of her grandmother's voice. She didn't sound one bit glad.

"What's the matter?" asked Evie. Her own voice sounded tight and foreign to her ears.

Gram frowned and sat forward on the edge of her chair. She was holding a long envelope in her hand.

"Pack yourself an overnight bag," she said. "Tomorrow, you and I are going on a little trip."

Chapter 15

The Way Life Should Be?

She had known as soon as she saw the envelope in Gram's hands. It was the letter, of course. The letter she'd written to her father. In her haste to get the letter mailed she'd forgotten the stamp. How stupid! How incredibly stupid! And so, when the letter came through the small local post office, they'd recognized the return address and brought it back. Back to Gram.

One look and Gram had figured it out. Now they were going to the hospital for a visit. Gram had insisted. "It's time," was all she'd said. Evie hadn't asked whether she'd read the letter. She was embarrassed that Gram had found out she'd written it behind her back.

But it would only be Gram and Evie going. The boys

weren't old enough, that's what Gram had said. Their father's brother, Uncle Gunnar, would be there to keep an eye on the boys and take care of the inn. Kirby had sulked and Jemmy had cried. And how was it that they weren't old enough to visit at the hospital? What did age have to do with it? And why, after all these years, were they paying him a visit now?

Evie looked back as Gram drove the car down the driveway. Kirby stood on the porch with his arms folded, his mouth pulled down at the corners. Uncle Gunnar stood beside him, as tall and straight and stern as ever. He had a square jaw, a straight, beaklike nose, and ice-blue eyes. He didn't smile often, but when he did it changed his whole face. When he smiled you could almost like him.

But he wasn't smiling now. He nodded goodbye, ignoring Jemmy, who was blubbering like a baby behind the screen door. Poor Jemmy. Both boys had argued right up to the last minute, still hoping to come along. But Gram had stood firm, and none of them dared cross her.

Evie didn't need to look up to know when they'd hit the main road—the crunch and spit of the gravel drive gave way to the smooth hum of the pavement. She sighed. It would be a long ride down the coast and into New Hampshire. They rode in awkward silence. There were too many questions, long buried, bubbling just below the surface of things. Every so often they'd bob up into Evie's head. She'd take a deep breath, but before she could form the words the question would sink back down into that deep, dark hiding place where she was used to stashing things—things that were better left alone.

Evie pulled out her sketch pad and flipped back the cover. Drawing might pass the time and fill in the gaps where there should have been conversation. She opened up a fresh page and started to doodle. "Opening up the channels" was what Julia called it—letting the pencil carry out ideas you never even knew were in your head.

Gram made an occasional comment, marking their progress by reading aloud the familiar road signs along the way.

" 'Bath Ironworks,' " she'd announce. " 'Home of the largest crane in the world.' " Or "Ayuh, 'Old Orchard Beach.' "

Evie nodded, acknowledging Gram's effort to fill the silence in the car. Then came her own personal favorite, plastered across a large blue billboard: WELCOME TO MAINE: THE WAY LIFE SHOULD BE! And it was true, life was pretty good in Maine. What she couldn't figure out was, if life was so good in Maine, why were they stirring things up by going to New Hampshire?

" 'Piscataqua Bridge—Caution: Crosswinds.' " Evie looked at Gram, with that determined look on her face, hunched up close to the steering wheel. Maybe she thought that forward angle would spare them from being blown off the bridge by those crosswinds.

"Well," said Gram finally, in that same stiff voice she'd been using since she'd announced the trip, "I suppose you have some questions."

It wasn't fair for her to ask like that. To force Evie to ask what she'd been encouraged to stifle for half her life. Evie sat there, silent, her lips clamped shut, tight as a clam.

Gram sighed. "It's my fault, of course. I know that now. But someone had to protect you. I did it the only way I knew how."

Protect you? What was she talking about? Hadn't they both been thinking about her father, about him being sick in that hospital? Evie blinked and stared out the window.

Gram cleared her throat. Evie could feel her glancing anxiously across the car at her, hoping she'd say something. Well, too bad. She couldn't think of a single word to say. It was as if the crosswinds on the bridge back there had blown any sensible words clear out of her head. Like she'd left her brains back in Maine, on the other side of the river.

"He couldn't handle it. Just couldn't handle it. When my Emily died, he just about died along with her. Godfrey Mighty, I never saw a man turn inside himself in grief like your father did."

Emily? Her mother, Gram's daughter, of course. Gram went on, but her words kind of floated around outside Evie's head. Gorry, her mind felt dull all of a sudden. *What* was she saying? The *drink* that got him? Evie shook her head and tried to concentrate.

Gram's voice rose a little. "It had *nothing* to do with you or the boys."

But she was wrong about that. It had *everything* to do

with them. As they pulled off the highway she glanced across the car at her grandmother.

Gram's eyes seemed to swim in the puddles that suddenly welled along the soft folds of her eyelids.

Evie bit her bottom lip. "Don't," pleaded a voice in her head, "please don't."

Too late. A tear spilled over the edge and ran down Gram's cheek. Evie shut her eyes and turned away. She would have liked to cover her ears with her hands, like Jemmy would have done.

But Gram went on. The sound of her voice frightened Evie. It sounded shaky and old.

"When Jemmy was born and Emily died, I needed to blame someone. Godfrey Mighty, things like that just shouldn't happen! His drinking away his grief made it easy for me to blame him."

Drinking away his grief? What was she saying, anyway? That Evie's father was a *drunk*? The car felt stuffy all of a sudden. Evie rolled the window down and let the air blow on her face. Her hair whipped across her cheeks. She didn't bother to push it back.

"And there'd been an accident. Your father had gotten hurt. That was the straw that broke the camel's back. So, when he couldn't take care of you anymore, I took the three of you to live with me. What else could I do? Things had been so bad for you there—all of six years old and trying to watch the boys and look after your father—well, it was too much for any child to bear!"

Evie didn't answer. It didn't require an answer. And it was a good thing too, because her mind still felt like it was working in slow motion. Gram's words knocked around her head like the lyrics to a long-forgotten song. As each word was spoken, Evie remembered a little bit more, a little bit more of what she'd thought she'd forgotten.

"And then, after you came to live with me, I tried to forgive Jerry, I really did." Gram shook her head, as if to convince herself of her sincerity. "By then he'd had a nervous breakdown and wound up in that hospital." She made small *tsk* sounds with her tongue and shook her head. "I knew it was only right for a father to have some contact with his children, sick or not. I'd dress you up and set out for a visit, but you didn't want to go. It was too safe over to the inn. It seemed to me you needed to forget, and so I let you. But I was wrong. And I'm sorry for it now."

Evie felt tears sting behind her eyelids. She knew she should say something to tell her grandmother it was okay. But she couldn't. Someday she would, but right now she couldn't.

They drove up a long driveway that cut through a rolling lawn scorched brown in the heat. A large white house stood on the hill, with several brick buildings behind it. They reminded Evie of school buildings, but without the construction paper flowers and butterflies decorating the windows.

Gram parked the car and they got out. A group of frail-looking people sat out front, many in wheelchairs. Some had sweaters on, or blankets across their laps, despite the heat. Most of them perked up when Evie and Gram approached, like puppies in the dog pound, each competing for a little attention. Evie looked away, embarrassed. Instead she focused on a big yellow dog lying there beside one of the old men. It thumped its thick tail at her and she bent to stroke its head. She was in no hurry to get inside.

"That's Sheba," said a young, smiley nurse who had just wheeled an old lady outside. She paused and scratched behind the old dog's ears. "Sheba lives here with Mr. Stuart." She smiled at the old man holding the leash. "He's great company for you, isn't he?" The old man didn't answer. Nurse Smiley didn't seem to notice. She glanced back at Evie. "You can't imagine how some of our patients benefit from a pet like Sheba."

Gram looked at Nurse Smiley. Evie knew that look. It was her "let's get down to business" look. Gram cleared her throat.

"We're here to see Jerry Johannson. Do you know where we can find him?"

"Sure, follow me. I'll take you up." They followed the nurse in silence up the stairs, down a narrow hallway, and up to a small room.

Nurse Smiley went in ahead and spoke in an extra loud, sugarcoated voice. "Look who's here, Jerry!"

It was the kind of voice Evie'd used with some of the tiny children visiting at the inn.

She could barely see him in the corner of the room,

sitting there with the shades drawn. In the dim light all she could make out was his shadow, a dim silhouette. She tried not to stare, but it was hard to tear her eyes away. Her eyes felt greedy to get a good look at him—to drink in the face she'd memorized from that photo.

The nurse motioned for them to step inside. Evie edged her way into the room. Then, feeling self-conscious, she forced her feet to take normal steps forward.

She thought she should say something to him, but her tongue felt thick and clumsy and her mind still seemed awfully slow. Gorry, what kind of visit was this, anyway? Why didn't he speak to her, for God's sake? Nurse Smiley slipped out the door and Gram took Evie by the elbow and steered her around the side of him.

"How've you been, Jerry?"

Gram's voice sounded like it belonged to someone else. Some stranger reading a line from a play or something. And there was no answer. Evie stared at him and he stared back. He didn't look anything like the picture—nothing like it at all. Looking at him was like looking at Uncle Gunnar, but a shrunken and watered-down version, blurred and worn out. Her eyes settled on the hair on the side of his head, all bunched and standing up every which way. It was exactly the same as Jemmy's when he'd slept on his cowlick the wrong way. She'd always thought it was cute on Jemmy, but seeing it on her father—on a grown-up man—made her feel sad and embarrassed. She forced her eyes away from his hair and concentrated on his face.

Gram went on, louder, as if he hadn't heard her. "Jerry, here's your Eva Jean. Evie, give your father a kiss."

Frozen. Her whole body was frozen. Gorry, she couldn't move an inch. He moved his mouth as if to say something, but no sound came out. It was like he was chewing away at the uncomfortable silence that was filling the whole room. Then, as if giving up on the words he couldn't manage, he motioned for her.

Slowly, he stretched one shaky hand toward her, those watery blue eyes looking right through her, right past her, at something else, at something no one else could see.

She couldn't help it—couldn't do a single thing about the peculiar sound that escaped from her mouth. Oh God, she just couldn't seem to stop it. And once it started it just kept coming—a gasping kind of cry. She slammed her hand over her mouth, and when that didn't stop the sound, she turned, pushed past Gram, and ran. She *had* to get out of there. Through the dark doorway, along the narrow hall, down the stairs, and out the front door. She stopped finally, and leaned back against the car door, crying and choking right out loud, just like Jemmy had been doing back home behind the screen door. She took a deep, shaky breath. She had to get hold of herself, she had to think. She began counting, "One hundred, ninety-nine, ninety-eight, ninety-seven . . . By ninety-six she could think more clearly.

It was those eyes of his, that look on his face. Godfrey Mighty, she'd seen that expression on *another* face, a face she'd tried hard to forget. No wonder Gram had never brought her here. She hadn't wanted her to know—of course, that was it. But now she knew all right, she could plainly see that her father, her *dad*, someone she was actually *related* to—had an awful lot in common with somebody else—with that madman back on the cliffs of Coleman's Cove. And the thought that he might have been better off dead, like her mother, crept up on her suddenly, and set her to crying all over again.

Chapter 16
Hurricane

The days after the visit to the hospital passed in a blur for Evie. Nothing—not the cat, which continued to hang around, not the madman out on the cliffs, not Bill and Julia's growing friendship, not even the cave paintings—seemed to interest her much.

"Come on, Evie," Michael pleaded. "Let's go out to the . . ." He wiggled his eyebrows behind his glasses. "Maybe there's another painting."

She was curious, but . . .

"Look," she said. "We know it was the madman who painted those pictures."

She'd finally put it all together—how he'd broken into the shed the night of the storm and taken some rags and other supplies that he needed. How he'd gone out and built the lean-to to keep his stuff in. And painted in between. Going back out there when the mystery was solved was somehow not as appealing. And besides, there was a storm blowing in. A big one. She nodded toward the window.

"What we ought to do is go out and fasten down the shutters. Kirby and Jemmy will have to drag in the porch wicker, too."

The sky had that unsettled pea-green tint that spelled a nasty summer storm. Most of the storms this early in the hurricane season just sort of bounced off Cape Cod and whirled out to sea, leaving coastal Maine with nothing more than a little wind and some heavy rain. But this time they wouldn't be so lucky. Already the leaves on the trees were whipping around in the wind, flipping back so that only their pale undersides were showing.

Her mood darkened with the threatening weather. The storm brewing reminded her of her trip with Gram—kind of hanging in the air between them, waiting to erupt. Since they'd gotten back they hadn't talked much about it. What was there to say, really? Evie wondered a hundred times why they had even bothered going. So that she could see her father for what he was?

The first fat drops of rain pelted against the window, and Evie sighed. They'd better tend to those shutters, and fast. She could hear the boys out on the porch, dragging the furniture over to the shed. Their voices were buffeted by the wind and thrown back and forth out of hearing. Gram was already leaning out the upstairs windows, pulling the shutters closed. Evie started down below and Michael followed.

She hoisted each window, leaned into the rain, and yanked at the tall green shutters, the wind whipping across her face. It was surprising how quickly the wind had gained strength. In a matter of minutes the weather had turned downright ugly. The next huge gust carried the boys' voices toward her again, high-pitched and agitated. Something in the tone of their voices forced her to lean out farther, despite the sting of the rain on her face and the force of the wind against the shutters.

Scraps of an argument were all she could make out. Jemmy whining and Kirby yelling. "Storm" was clear, and "rocks." What were they carrying on about, anyway?

The wind suddenly grabbed the edge of the shutter from her hand and slammed it back, pinching the fleshy part of her thumb against the house.

"Ouch!" she yelled. Michael pulled her back in and secured the shutter himself. Evie sucked on her sore thumb and shook it to ease the sting. She should have been paying attention to what she was doing. Enough listening to their nonsense. It was time to finish with the shutters, take out the candles, and hole up in the kitchen. Wet and cranky, they dripped across the kitchen to the next window and the next until all the downstairs windows were closed off. The shutters blocked out what was left of the late-afternoon light and rattled against the window frames like clattering skeletons. Even the kitchen looked dark and creepy on a day like this.

As she wiped her forehead with a dish towel, a peculiar commotion cut through the roar of the wind outside. Evie and Michael exchanged looks and made their way toward the sound, down the main hall and into the parlor.

Julia stood at the front door, the wind viciously rattling the screen and sending furious sheets of rain across the wooden floor. She was soaked to the skin.

"Jemmy went out toward the rocks!" Julia gasped. "He went out after the cat, and Kirby followed him."

"I sent Pop after them," she added, "and Bill's gone with him."

That cat! It was true, the omen in her dream. Now the boys were in danger, *real* danger, on account of that cat! She should have paid closer attention to their arguing. It was the cat they'd been talking about, she was sure of it. Evie grabbed her slicker from the closet just as the Elliots made their way down the stairs, wide-eyed and nervous.

"You're not going anywhere," said Gram, waving her finger in Evie's direction.

"The men went out already, Evie!" Julia yelled. "There's nothing else you can do!" Evie heard the women screaming after her, but she ignored them. She threw her weight against the screen door and ran out into the storm. Michael followed her. She could hear the Elliots calling to him. But they both went on out. There was nothing else to do.

She could see Pop and Bill in the distance, way out by the woods. They called to them, but their voices were lost in the storm. They gave up yelling and concentrated on running through the wind. It felt a little like walking through the sea, against the waves. And they were almost as wet as if they had been. It was the first time that she really felt grateful to have Michael beside her.

Her thoughts turned to the cat—still causing trouble for them even after she'd repeatedly sent him away. A chill ran down her spine as she thought about his thin little body, his white fur drenched in the rain. The chill spread as her thoughts turned to the boys. One wrong move, one tiny slip, and they could tumble from the rocks and into the sea. If she had known, if she had had *any* idea that Jemmy would try something this stupid, she would have found a way, some way, to keep the cat.

They caught up with Bill and Pop, finally, and Evie tugged at Bill's sleeve. He turned to her, breathing heavily, the rain splashing across his eyeglasses. He yelled at her, words she couldn't make out. She knew what he meant, though. He was scolding them for following. She ignored him, pushed ahead a bit, and fell in beside Pop.

Finally they reached the place where the trees leaned back and the rocks took over. The wind seemed doubly strong there. They'd have to move ahead slowly. She scanned the rocks. The sky, rocks, and water seemed to blur together—one cold, wet sheet of gray. There was no hint of yellow raincoats or red boots anywhere.

They pressed on, over the summit and around to the

other side. She nearly lost her footing several times, and even Pop was slowing down. Godfrey Mighty, *where were those boys?*

And then she spotted something. A small blur over at the farthest tip of rock. A dot of color clinging on at the edge of the overhang. She called their names, even though they'd never hear her. She began to run, leaving the others behind.

It seemed like a slow-motion scene from a movie—every step she took was thwarted by the wind, making her journey to the cliff twice as long as it should have taken.

It was them, all right, hunched together at the edge of the rocks, just above her pine ladder. They saw her coming and looked up as though they'd been expecting her all along. But even through the pelting rain she could see the tears on Jemmy's cheeks. He was pointing wildly into the space below them. Kirby held him back, a fierce expression on his face. Evie stumbled up to them and grabbed hold. She had to move them away from the edge, away from the steep drop of solid granite.

Jemmy pulled away from her. She had the urge to slap him silly. What was the matter with him? He'd get the three of them killed, yanking away like that, so close to the edge. She was about to scream at him, but as she looked his way she noticed something. Something small and white.

It was the cat, soaked to the skin, perched on a limb of the pine ladder, just below their reach. Oh God, how could they leave the poor thing there like that? How long could it hold on in this wind? She pushed the boys back and lay down flat. She reached down toward the shivering animal. Not close enough. Evie inched forward and tried again. It was impossible.

Something moved below her. Something besides the surging waves at the bottom of the cave. She squinted through the rain to make it out. Up, slowly up, came a hand on the ladder. Hand over hand he eased himself up, until he was just below the cat.

His eyes met hers and for a moment the only things she saw were those eyes of his, so blue, and so frightening. Only this time there was life in the madman's eyes. Life, and something else. Something like concern or kindness. He turned his eyes to the cat, and with one shove, he pushed him up and into her hands.

Evie grabbed the cat and shoved the boys away from the edge to safety. The others had arrived and Pop threw himself on the ground facedown and extended a hand to the madman. Bill held Pop's legs with all his might. Evie cradled the shivering cat in one arm, and held the boys back with the other.

All Evie could see was his hand, hanging on to Pop's. Then there was a crash. Bill was yanking Pop away from the edge. Evie rushed over, half-blinded by the rain.

The pine was gone! Gone! She strained her eyes against the gray swirl of rock and sea. The waves had come crashing in, and the slate-colored, whitecapped water looked like it was boiling between the rocks. And there, for just an instant, she caught sight of the pine, bobbing in the water like a toy boat in a bathtub with the madman hanging on for dear life.

She had to get help. She thrust the cat into Bill's arms as he struggled to maneuver the boys back toward the woods. Michael ran behind her. How long could the madman survive in that raging sea? And what about Pop? Would he try to get down there and rescue the man? These thoughts drove her on. Michael ran in to call the police and Evie ran to the shed. It would take the police too long to get there. Way too long. The door on the shed had broken off its hinges again. She ran in, yanked the sturdy lobster line and a life preserver out of the corner, and ran back out to the rocks.

By the time they'd heaved him out of the water, the police had arrived. They wrapped his waterlogged body in a warm blanket. At first Evie thought he was dead, but as they lifted the stretcher, he turned his head and opened his eyes. He extended his hand toward her and for a second their eyes met. Then they carried him off.

Chapter 17
Unfinished Business

The police were there when they returned. Evie told them about the madman and they had about a thousand questions about him, spoken and unspoken. Who was the man on the rocks? *Was it true that she really didn't know him?* How many times had she seen him before? *Why hadn't she told her grandmother about him?*

She could feel her eyes starting to droop. She was exhausted—not just her body, but her brain as well. Gram sent them all off finally, telling them in no uncertain terms that Evie needed to be tucked into bed. The Elliots looked positively shell-shocked, and took Michael upstairs with them like a family of zombies. As Gram took her up to bed Evie heard the heavy boots and hushed voices of the policemen heading out the door and back into the storm. She took one last look at the cat, snuggled in a small box beside the stove.

The last thing she remembered was Gram's soft hands, smelling, as always, of oil paint and linseed oil, smoothing her damp hair off of her face and arranging the bed covers around her chin. She was safe now, back home at the inn, in her grandmother's care. In less time than she could count, she fell asleep.

She should have known better. She should have left a candle lit, *anything* to ward off that dream. It hit her hard, harder than it usually did. It seemed that she was dreaming with all five senses.

She felt the crash as well as heard it. Then she was running toward the dining room, toward Kirby's cries. She had promised to take care of him, she had promised. But that bird was in her way. Growing, looming over her, grabbing at her with those sharp talons. She screamed, and the bird changed, grew, hardened into the table, metallic feet grasping those crystal balls. She could see her own face reflected in the balls, distorted and overblown. She could see the terror in her eyes and the tears on her cheeks. She looked away. Toward her brother. Her brother needed her.

This time she saw him howling in his high chair. His back was arched and he pushed his small feet with all his might, struggling to free himself and slip out of the chair. He was tugging at the tablecloth and pointing toward the floor.

She was on her knees in an instant, crawling under the

table. The claw feet stood guard as Kirby's feet kicked in their chair in front of her.

And there, in a heap next to her was her father. The bottle in his hand was smashed and the strong odor of the rusty-colored liquid stung her nose. His eyes were blank, unseeing, and he moaned with pain. It had been him all along who had fallen from his chair. She shook him, hard. Wake up. Why wouldn't he wake up? Pull him, she had to pull him out from under the table. God, he was so heavy. On her hands and knees she dragged him. But wait, Daddy was waking up. Blue eyes, his blue eyes stared up at her.

Suddenly the image changed. The face, her father's face, blurred and became another face. And she found herself on the floor under that hateful table with the madman. He pulled himself up on one elbow and handed her the cat. Then water, gray, whitecapped water poured into the room, under the table, washing him away from her.

She awoke with a start, gasping for air. And she knew. She remembered it now. How her drunken father slipped out of his chair and collapsed under the table. How she'd grabbed baby Jemmy in her arms and Kirby by the hand and run to the neighbors. How the ambulance had come and taken her father away. How desperate she'd been to forget it all. And how Gram had come and erased it all away.

Evie sat up, a numbing calm settling heavily on her. A bit of sun shone through the slats of the shutters. So that was it, after all. The dream didn't seem as scary as it had before. Grim—but no longer scary. Because this time it had an ending to it. And knowing the ending, even a *rotten* ending, was better than waiting for it to hit you smack in the gut every time you went to sleep.

So she finally saw her father clearly. Somewhere, deep down, she had known all along.

Chapter 18
Clive Aaron Thompson

They were all sitting around the kitchen table—Gram, the boys, Julia, Bill, Pop, and the Elliots. The coffee was on, and Evie could smell the blueberry muffins baking in the oven. The storm had raged for more than twenty-four hours, and she had slept through more than half of it. The quiet conversation in the kitchen came to a halt when she entered the room.

"Good morning," Gram said to Evie. Gram inhaled deeply, and pulled her mouth back in that straight line that signaled a problem. As she poured Evie a cup of coffee, Mr. Elliot pulled back a chair and motioned for her to sit.

Evie sat down and looked from one to the other. Mrs.

Elliot lowered her eyes and excused herself from the table. Mr. Elliot followed. Even the boys seemed shy, nodding a little and making their way out the back door with Julia and Bill. Pop cleared his throat and got up. "Think I'll go tend to that hinge on the shed," he said. Gram sighed.

"I know you'll want to see this," she said. She placed the newspaper in front of Evie. Evie looked over the photographs of the storm damage. It had been wicked bad. She glanced up at her grandmother.

"Bottom of the page," Gram said. She looked down, but Evie didn't miss the deepening of that crease in her brow. Her hands felt clammy as she folded back the page and scanned down. Her heart dropped. There it was:

STORM BRINGS ONE FATALITY

Evie looked up. Gram nodded. "I'm sorry," she said.

What an odd thing to say. But Evie realized that she felt sorry as well. She bit her lip and read on.

> COLEMAN'S COVE—Local police reported one fatality attributed to yesterday's storm. The victim has been identified as **Clive Aaron Thompson,** age 54. He had reportedly fallen into the water during the height of the storm. Several residents, including a 12-year-old girl, were successful in pulling Mr. Thompson from the water. He later

died at Coleman General Hospital. Mr.
Thompson was remembered by many local
residents as a renowned painter of numerous highly regarded land- and seascapes of
the upper Maine Coast. His works have
been shown in galleries across the U.S. Little has been heard about Mr. Thompson in
recent years. It is believed that he gave up
painting and spent the last years of his life
in seclusion.

He hadn't given up painting! Evie felt angry all of a
sudden. He might have been a crazy man, living all alone
out there between those rocks. But crazy had nothing to
do with talent. And it had nothing to do with compassion.
She looked at the cat napping in the corner. That madman had not only saved the cat—it was likely that he'd
saved her brothers too. She had no doubt that they would
have tried to rescue Robinson out there. She closed her
eyes to block out the image of the boys falling into that
furious gray water.

"You did all you could, Evie," said Gram softly. "You've
always been a child that did all you could and more. I'm
very, very proud of you."

Evie thought for a moment about Gram's words. It
seemed that doing all she could do was never quite
enough. Not enough to save her father from his grief. Not
enough to save the madm—no, to save Mr. Thompson.

Evie held the coffee cup in both hands and let the warmth flow through her. She took the last sip and placed the cup back in the saucer.

Gram picked up the cup and moved toward the stove. She scooped a small spoonful of soomp out of the pot and handed the cup back to Evie.

"Turn the cup around," said Gram. Evie hesitated. Gram nodded slowly and repeated her words to Evie, more forcefully this time.

"Turn the cup around."

Evie rolled her eyes as she swirled the cup impatiently in her hands. Would Gram *ever* give up on her fortune-telling? She didn't much feel like playing along. What for? All that nonsense about good luck, bright futures, and the best one of all—being born lucky. Evie nearly laughed out loud as she thought back to all the times Gram had read *that* one in her cup. Jeez, if being born lucky meant having your mother die and your father turn into a drunk, what in the world happened to kids who were born *un*-lucky? Maybe they turned out like poor old C A T—Clive Aaron Thompson.

As she turned the cup over to drain, Gram looked at her sharply.

"I know what you're thinking," she said, "and you're *wrong*."

Evie shrugged. "It's just that you only look at the good stuff! What's the point of telling fortunes if you don't look at the rotten stuff too?"

"So, you think I only look at the good stuff?" Gram's

voice took on a tight sound. It matched the expression on her face. "Well, young lady, if you think I don't see the whole picture, you are very, *very* wrong."

Gorry, it was hard to believe Gram was getting so worked up again over this stupid fortune-telling thing.

"You know, Evie," she said, "I've learned a bit in these last six years. When I was younger, it was true, I only saw what I wanted to see. I'd ignore everything else." She tapped Evie on the arm. "And I've noticed that I did a remarkable job of passing *that* talent along to *you*."

Evie's face grew hot and she looked away. Why didn't Gram just tell the silly fortune and get it over with? Evie thrust the cup at Gram. But Gram didn't seem to notice.

"Here's the thing," said Gram, leaning in toward her. "You want to be smart in this life? You want to be happy? Well, intelligence comes from keeping your eyes wide open. Face things head-on, that's what you have to do. But Evie . . . that won't bring you happiness. Life hands you too many problems. Happiness comes from learning to look at things in the best possible light. Like painting a beautiful picture. It's a question of where you decide to focus your attention."

She took Evie's cup in her hands. "When I look in this cup, I see a clump of grounds. I might not like the looks of them. They might spell trouble. So you know what I do? I turn the cup around another way, until I see something better in it."

Evie snuck a look in Gram's direction.

"Here," Gram said, thrusting the cup into Evie's hands,

"take a sharp look at everything life's handed you. Then think hard, and decide for yourself the best way to look at it. *Choose* your fortune, Evie—because whatever it is you decide to focus on—well, that's exactly what life'll hand you."

Evie took the cup in her hands and stared at the soomp inside. She closed her eyes for a moment, looked back at the designs in the cup, and slowly, deliberately, turned the cup around.

Chapter 19
The Eye of the Beholder

The Elliots' car was pulled right up to the porch. Mr. Elliot ran back and forth with the suitcases while his wife gave him a steady stream of directions about the best way to pack the car. Bill, Julia, and Pop stood on the porch, saying goodbye to the Elliots. Kirby and Jemmy ran between them all, causing a good-natured commotion.

Evie walked around to face Michael, who was standing there stroking the cat. It was hard to believe that he was leaving. And even harder to believe that she would miss him. But she would. She really would. She suddenly felt shy. She couldn't think of a thing to say.

"It's okay," he said. "We'll be back next summer." He pushed his dark hair out of his eyes and kicked at the gravel with his foot. Evie smiled at him. For once, he was embarrassed.

"We can write," Evie said.

Michael grinned at her. "Yeah," he said, "if you remember to put a stamp on the envelope."

She poked him with her elbow.

Robinson curled around her ankles.

"Are you sure we can't take him off your hands?" asked Mr. Elliot, pointing toward the cat.

"And if they don't take him," called Bill from the porch, "I might be persuaded."

Pop shook his head. "Crazy people spend half the summer fighting about getting rid of the cat and the rest of the summer fighting over who's to keep 'im."

It had been Bill who'd pointed out that the cat was deaf. Something about white cats with two different-colored eyes—some genetic problem, was what he'd said. Of course, it made sense after he'd mentioned it.

Evie smiled. "He'll be in good hands, I promise you." She handed Michael a sketch. Even behind his hanging-down hair and thick glasses she could see that he was delighted. Evie had worked very hard on it. First, at Julia's urging, she'd concentrated on the negative spaces around the cat, then, at Gram's suggestion, she'd plumped him up, smoothed him out, and prettied him up, for beauty's sake. The result was nearly perfect, and Evie was proud of it. She had almost decided to keep it herself as a reminder of the amazing little animal. Something to remember him by when he was gone.

146

They waved as the Elliots pulled away, and as usual, Bill and Julia headed out toward the rocks. They'd become more than just friends, and Evie had the feeling that by the time autumn came they'd be seeing either a lot more of Bill or a lot less of Julia.

"Well," said Gram, "that's that. Now, let's get our own car packed up so we can get on our way."

They waved to Pop, who would be keeping an eye on things while they were gone. He nodded and tipped his blue cap to say goodbye.

It was a noisier trip down the coast this time, with the boys arguing and talking in the backseat. Evie'd let Jemmy hold the cat. After all, it had been hard to convince him that Robinson would have a good home in New Hampshire with their father. He'd cried a little, but the idea of bringing his daddy so precious a gift had won out.

She held a few gifts of her own in her hands—she held the small carved elephant gingerly. You could hardly see the glue along its upturned trunk. Soon it would have a windowsill all to itself.

"It's a lovely picture." Gram was glancing sideways at the paper in Evie's lap. Evie nodded. It *was* a good picture—a picture of the way life should be. A fantasy, of course, but it didn't matter. It was a picture of her mother and father, smiling, just as they had been in that photograph. But there were three others in the picture—Kirby, Jemmy, and Evie herself.

They were getting close now. Before long the boys would meet their father again.

Evie turned to them in the backseat.

"Remember," she said, "he's not feeling well. Don't expect him to say much. Not with his mouth, at least."

Gram nodded her approval. She'd been worried about how the boys would react. Evie went on. She'd rehearsed it a thousand times. "He'll probably just stare at you, and you know what that means?" She paused. They looked at her solemnly. "It means he's talking to you with his eyes—telling you how much he loves you and memorizing you so he can see you when you're gone."

Maybe it was true, after all.

They parked the car and the boys scrambled out. They stared at the buildings set up on the hill.

"All right," said Gram, "here we are."

Evie got out of the car then, took a deep breath, and led the way inside.

ABOUT THE AUTHOR

Barbara Mariconda, author of two previous chapter books for young readers, lives with her husband, two teenagers, and one very large poodle in Stratford, Connecticut. Besides being a writer, Barbara is a teacher and musician who loves to travel, particularly to coastal Maine.